VIKING CLAIMED

VIKING CLAIMED

THE TRIAD SERIES, BOOK 4

KATE PEARCE

PROLOGUE

THE TRIAD SYSTEM

"Aki... you aren't even trying."

Aki looked across the room at his twin brother, Einarr. "Trying to what?"

"Learn."

Aki shoved back his chair and rose to his feet. "Because it doesn't interest me." He gazed longingly out of the window into the darkness of the strange planet he now inhabited. "I want to be outside. I want to go *home*."

Behind him his brother sighed in a way that had begun to infuriate Aki greatly.

"There is no home, you know that."

Aki swung around, his braided blond hair catching his cheek. "How do you know? We could be bewitched. The Gods could be lying to us."

"For what purpose?" Einarr stretched out his long legs and tried to look relaxed, but Aki wasn't fooled. "You have seen the pictures. The Earth is completely changed beyond our wildest dreams."

"It could be a lie."

"Again I ask you why would anyone want to lie to us? We

defrosted four thousand years too late. We should be grateful that these people have welcomed us into their world and are trying to help us even when you are being so pigheaded."

"I am not being pigheaded." Aki glared at his twin. "But then I am not the fool who thinks he's found his mate and *wants* all this to be true."

Einarr rose slowly to his feet, his blue eyes narrowed. "Are you questioning my honor, brother?"

Aki reached forward and poked Einarr's broad chest. "You won't even fight with me anymore. Your female has your cock in a stranglehold."

Einarr's gaze went stony. "My female is thousands of miles away on a different planet."

Aki pushed him again, making him rock back on his heels. "Is that why you are in such a foul mood?"

"At least I have a reason." Einarr shoved him back. "You, on the other hand, are just contrary. *Halfviti!*"

"*Kukalabbi!*" With a growl Aki launched himself at his brother. To his surprise, his challenge was met and accepted, and within seconds they were rolling around on the floor, desks and chairs and equipment falling around them as they tried to choke and punch the other into inglorious surrender.

An alarm blared somewhere, and Aki was pulled off his brother by two of the security team that accompanied them everywhere. Einarr looked up at him, his mouth bloody.

"As I said, you are a fool, a halfwit. The longer you take to complete this task, the longer we have to stay here on this Mitan moon. I want to go to Pavlovan."

Aki tried to shrug off Brown and Ilker, the two men who held his arms tightly behind his back. "You can get a female here."

The sound Einarr made was almost inhuman as he struggled against the guards. "I want *my* female. If you do not care who or what you fuck, Aki, stay here. I swear to the Gods that I will finish the tasks assigned to me and leave you behind." He glanced up at his guards. "You can let me go now. I will not touch him. I am done with him."

"Release him," Brown, the head of security spoke up.

Einarr stood, and after one last glare at Aki, walked out, slamming the door behind him.

Brown sighed as he surveyed the wrecked room. "Ross, keep an eye on Einarr and get someone here to clean up again." He dropped his hold on Aki's right arm. "And you'd better get a grip. Did you just call your twin a scumbag?" Brown tapped his earpiece. "That's the closest translation I could get. What the frak was that all about?"

"My brother is a lovesick fool."

"Your brother has completed his onworld training and is about to leave you here and go to another planet. Is that what you want?"

Aki shook off the second guard and swiped at his face. His nose appeared to be bleeding and two of his teeth felt loose. Experimentally, he cracked his jaw and winced.

"I want to go home."

"You won't be going anywhere if you don't pass Reintegration 101," Brown stated. "Our scientists would love that."

"What do you mean?" Aki turned to survey the chief of security who wasn't known for his sweetness of tongue or his inability to pull a punch.

"If you don't get with the program, FREN will be suggesting you aren't capable of dealing with your new world and need to be closely watched by our scientists. You think you're in a cage now, mate, you wait until you see what they do to you."

Aki kicked a chair. "This 'work' you expect me to do makes no sense. It does not *test* me. I already know who and what I am. I am a *warrior*."

"You can be a warrior in the bloody Pavlovan army if you want, but you've still got to pass the tests."

"Brown, you bore me."

"Just trying to get the idea through your four-thousand-year-old thick skull." Brown headed for the door. "There are always wars to fight, Viking, you will still be needed, but—"

"First I have to pass the stupid tests," Aki finished for him.

"Do you want to go to the infirmary and get your jaw checked out?"

"It is fine."

Brown sighed. "Bloody stubborn Viking idiot."

Aki picked up one of the chairs and set it in front of the table with the white screen on it. He sat down and the screen came to life. The thought of any scientists getting near him and treating him like a worthless dog was enough to help him concentrate.

The voice in the box started speaking and for the first time, Aki sighed and paid attention.

1

"Do you really think he's coming?"

Elli Slavin glanced at the tense face of her friend Frey as she watched the exit doors of the spaceport open and close on an endless stream of people.

"Of course he is." Elli glanced over her shoulder. "Senator Ash has just arrived so I'd say it was a certainty."

"He offered to put Einarr and Aki up in his apartment. He already has a group of telepathic human soldiers living there who came to Pavlovan with Neeve's First Male. He thought the Vikings might feel more comfortable being with a group of men who are also learning to acclimatize to Pavlovan culture." Frey sighed. "Gods, I'm babbling now, aren't I? What if Einarr has forgotten me? Or regrets our bond or…"

The doors opened again and two huge males emerged, one blond the other dark. With a shriek, Frey ran across the concourse and launched herself at the dark-haired Viking who picked her up as if she weighed nothing and kissed the life out of her.

"I don't think he's forgotten you, Frey," Elli murmured as the other Viking, the blond, navigated around his twin and came straight for her, a scowl on his handsome face. He wore his long hair loose around his shoulders apart from three small braids on his left temple.

She couldn't have moved even if a wall had been about to crush her as his vivid blue gaze scanned her face.

"Female."

His voice was deep and made her feel very female indeed. She stuck out her hand. "I'm Elli Slavin. We have met before."

"I remember it well." He took her hand and bowed over it before bringing it to his lips. "It is a pleasure, my lady."

She wanted to giggle and flutter her eyelashes at him.

She never giggled.

Turning slightly, she gestured at Ash, who was walking toward them. "My cousin, Senator Ash, is here to welcome you to Pavlovan. You will be staying with him."

"We have also met before. He is a powerful mind talker."

"Yes, he is quite exceptional." She risked a glance up at the Viking's austere face. His cheekbones were to die for and his eyes as blue as the Pavlovan oceans...

"You have this gift as well."

Gods if she'd thought his speaking voice was compelling, his thoughts were even more intimate.

"Pretty much everyone on Pavlovan is telepathic."

"But not quite like you."

"Aki Bloodaxe." Ash bowed. "Welcome to Pavlovan. As soon as your twin stops kissing his female, we can be on our way."

Aki scowled. "Then we had best settle in. I fear he means to kiss her all night."

"He'll need more privacy at some point." Ash smiled. "Perhaps you might mention that to him."

AKI SENT Einarr the thought and was relieved to see his twin pay attention for once and come closer, one hand joined with his mate's. Both of them were grinning like besotted fools.

Aki went to follow Ash out, and then realized Elli Slavin was saying something that sounded like a farewell.

"If you like, I'll come and say hi once you are settled in at Ash's. It's been so nice to see you again, and I hope—"

He took hold of her elbow. "You are coming with me."

"But I don't think—"

He met her anxious brown gaze. "Please."

"Are you sure?" She bit down on her lip and he found himself staring avidly at the small indentation her teeth had left. He wanted to lean down and lick that small groove before it disappeared, and then replace it with his own teeth, marking her as his own.

Her cheeks flushed, and he wondered how much she'd picked up of his curiously errant thought. Lifting her hand to his mouth he slowly bit down on the fleshy mound below her thumb. Her whole body quivered and her breathing hitched. Were all females on this planet so susceptible to a man's touch, or was he the problem? He hadn't touched a real woman for four thousand years...

"Aki?"

He looked up to see that Einarr and Frey had reached the exit.

"Come with me, Elli Slavin."

She sighed. "Okay."

The vehicle Ash led them into was large and appeared to need no horses to make it work. Since being catapulted into a different time and space, Aki had seen many wonders. He tried not to think about them too much or else his longing for his home overtook him. The idea that he could never go back, never kiss his little sister or his mother, or live the life he had always assumed would be his was terrifying.

Beside him, Elli shifted in her seat, her worried gaze fastened on his face. How many of his thoughts was he inadvertently sharing with her right now? He still hadn't learned to shield his mind very well. It hadn't been necessary at home when only he, Einarr and a handful of their male relatives had the power of mind talking. Here, he felt other people's thoughts beating constantly at him like raindrops.

"Are you all right, Aki?"

He looked down at her. "Aye. This is all a little strange still. That is all."

"I should imagine it must be quite a shock." She shivered. "If I'd been in your place, I think I would've gone mad."

His smile was grim. "I have considered it. But Einarr was there to guide me. I am lucky to have him."

He looked over at his twin whose mind was now so entangled with his female's that Aki might as well not have existed.

Elli gave him a sympathetic glance. "The first few months of a newly mated pair can be a bit intense. Your brother will be more like his old self once he has gotten through this first mating phase."

"I hope so," Aki grumbled. "He is behaving like a lovesick calf."

Ash who was sitting opposite Aki chuckled. "I was just as bad when Esca came to my bed and even worse when we completed our triad and found Soreya."

"You bed both of them?" Aki inquired.

"Yes."

"Good." His gaze moved back to Elli who was still watching him. She was very beautiful, her hair the rich yellow-red of gold and her skin freckled. He wondered how far down her body the freckles went...

Her cheeks flushed and she swallowed hard. Were his thoughts that obvious to every female on this planet? He would have to be more careful.

"Where are we going, Ash?" Aki asked.

"To my apartment. I have a large duplex within the building that's spread over two floors and three levels. I live in one suite with Esca and Soreya and the floor beneath that is for our guests."

The words made no sense, but Aki persevered. "Who else is there?"

Ash sat forward, his hands clasped together between his knees, his almost white hair streaming over his shoulder. "Currently, there's a group of ex-military telepaths from Earth."

"My planet?" Aki still found the idea that his world was not the only one ridiculous, but he'd learned to hide it. "Are they as old as Einarr and I am?"

"No one is as old as you two. They only arrived recently on Pavlovan." Ash hesitated. "They were in danger from their own government on Earth, so we offered them a home. Most of them intend to stay here and join the Pavlovan military."

Aki nodded. "Good. They sound like excellent companions. I like to fight."

"So do they. Their commander will enjoy matching his strength to yours."

Aki instinctively flexed his biceps and caught the flash of interest from Elli. He smiled at her. "Do you like to fight, Elli?"

A sudden image rushed into his head of her naked in his arms as they fought their way through an intense fucking. His cock hardened and he sat upright, his gaze locked on hers as he realized the salacious image had come from her.

She immediately averted her gaze and stared out of the window. Beside her Ash patted her knee.

"You have embarrassed my cousin." Ash's voice echoed inside Aki's head. *"I've never seen her react so violently to a male's presence before."*

"Do all Pavlovan females act like this around men?" Aki asked.

"Not unless they are extremely attracted to them." Ash winked at

him. *"My cousin isn't mated yet, so please feel free to pursue her if you have a genuine interest in mating with her. However, if you just want to fuck around, leave her alone."*

There was a threat behind Ash's politely spoken request that Aki intended to respect. He nodded. *"By Odin's blood, I swear I will never disrespect your kinswoman, Ash."*

"Good. I'd hate to have to set Esca on you." Ash looked out of the window as the vehicle slowed down. "We're here."

Aki got out and stared upward at the towering buildings that surrounded him. He tried not to let his jaw drop, but it was hard to understand the landscape he now found himself in. There were people everywhere, metal vehicles both large and small screaming through the sky and on the ground. And the noise... He wanted to cover his ears and cower in a corner like a small child caught in a raid.

"Aki?"

A gentle touch on his arm had him spinning around to face Elli.

"Are you ready to go inside?"

He nodded and allowed her to take his hand and lead him into the relative quietness of the stone building and into a small glass box that shot upward at such a speed that he thought he might puke up his innards. When the doors opened, he stumbled out only to find himself faced with a view over the whole town, which stretched for miles and miles in every direction. At least it wasn't as bad as the blackness of space.

Inside the room, a large man rose to greet them. His expression was pleasant, but Aki knew a fellow warrior when he saw one. To his surprise the man dropped down on one knee in front of Ash and kissed his hand.

"First Male."

"Second. I'm glad you're back, Esca. I want to introduce you to Einarr and Aki, Viking mind talkers from Earth."

Esca stood, his face on level with Aki's and stared at him.

"You must be Aki." He held out his hand. "I am very pleased to meet you."

Aki extended his hand as he'd learned to do. "How did you know which man I am?"

"Because I can feel the bond between your brother and his mate." Esca grinned. "And they obviously can't keep their hands off each other."

Aki looked back to see Einarr's female clinging to his side like a vine. Both of them were smiling and looked dazed with happiness.

"He is a fool."

"Why is that?" Esca asked.

"Because he needs to be more aware of what is going on around him. Anyone could come up and kill him and he would never even notice."

"Not in this apartment. Ash is a very important man and this building is guarded night and day." He looked over at Ash, who was listening to them intently. "And I would not let anyone hurt my First Male. I would die for him."

Aki nodded, impressed by the sincerity in Esca's voice. Perhaps there were a few worthy men on this planet after all.

Ash patted Esca's arm. "Let's hope it doesn't come to that," he murmured. "Would you like something to eat, Aki, or would you prefer to be shown to your quarters first?"

"I think my brother needs to find somewhere to fuck his female, and I would like to wash."

Einarr gave him a dirty look, but Aki merely smiled at him. His brother was usually very discreet when he took a woman, but not with the Pavlovan.

"Is it acceptable to fuck in front of others?" He directed the thought at Elli who had come to stand beside him.

She blushed again. *"Within one's Triad, yes, but in public? Usually only at the festivals at the Temple of the Oracle."*

"I would like to meet this Oracle." Aki murmured. "She is a powerful seer, is she not?"

Ash nodded. "Once you have settled in, I intend to take you and Einarr to visit her. She rarely comes to the city anymore. It doesn't suit her."

"I can understand why." Aki risked another quick glance at the sheer drop beneath the glass window. "There are too many mind talkers here. It makes my head ache."

Ash patted his arm. "You'll get used to it. We have teachers here who can help you protect your thoughts and distance you from others."

"More teachers?" Aki groaned.

"It would be worth your time to learn these things."

"If you say so," Aki said dubiously.

"Shall we go downstairs then?" Esca asked. "You get on with your work, Ash, I'll get them settled, and we'll all come back for a celebratory dinner."

AKI LIKED ESCA. Even his thoughts were straight as an arrow. He also *said* what he thought, which was just how Aki was. With a man like that, you knew where you were. He couldn't imagine what kind of female would appeal to both Ash and Esca. Would she be a tall, well-muscled warrior like one of his goddesses? He imagined the three of them fucking...

"Aki?"

Esca held open yet another door for him. Einarr and his female had gone straight to bed, and Elli had stayed back to talk to Ash about something. The door opened out into a large room with several seats around it, and one of the huge moving screens that he still struggled to comprehend. He inhaled the smell of roasting fowl and ale and immediately felt more relaxed. Outside the big glass windows, there were a group of men throwing some kind of ball at each other. The game involved many skirmishes away from the ball, which resulted in bodies flying everywhere.

"Watch out guys!"

Aki instinctively ducked as the ball flew toward the glass, but it bounced off and disappeared over the edge of the building.

"You dickhead, Rolf!" Two of the men were looking down over the parapet. "I hope you haven't killed anyone on the street. Even Ash would have a problem explaining that away."

For the first time in a long while, Aki found himself grinning. Ash was right; these were the kind of men who might understand him.

Esca banged on the glass and several faces turned toward him. Aki remained close to the door as the men filed in, each of them giving him an assessing glance as they greeted Esca.

"You're one of the Vikings Ash told us about." The tall redheaded male who'd lost the ball stepped forward. "Which one are you?"

"I am Aki."

"Good to meet you. I'm Rolf. Where's your brother?"

"Fucking." Aki shrugged. "He has a mated female."

"Lucky bastard." The huge blond muttered. He held out his hand. "I'm Kaiden. I'm in command of this motley crew."

Aki had to take a step back to take in all of Kaiden's huge frame. His muscles rivaled Aki's and his eyes were the color of steel.

The other man continued talking. "This here is Roberts, and that's Bevan, and the short-but-deadly one is Declan."

The other men nodded at him, their gazes assessing, their minds closed to him. Aki didn't mind that. He already had a headache from too much mind sharing from Einarr and Ash.

"You are from Earth?" Aki asked.

"Yes. We're all ex-military." Kaiden glanced at the other men. "We're pretty damn bored stuck in here, but like you, we have a lot to learn about Pavlovan culture before they let us loose on society."

"Do you not wish to return to Earth?"

Kaiden's smile was rueful. "They'd kill us. We are too formidable for them to control. We frightened them."

Aki nodded. "Sometimes that happened to my family. We had powerful magic, which made the weak fearful or eager to try and steal it for themselves."

Kaiden gestured toward the interior of the room. "Have some beer and Pavlovan chicken. It's not bad. Ash says once we are settled we can import stuff from Earth if we really want home cooking."

"I would like to return to my Earth." Aki confessed as he took the bottle Kaiden offered him. "But Einarr says it is gone."

"That must seem wrong to you."

Aki looked behind him where the man called Rolf had taken a seat. Despite his menacing appearance, Rolf's eyes were a soft golden brown and sympathy flowed from him like a warm spring.

"Sometimes I cannot believe it is true." Aki drank the entire bottle of ale in one gulp. "I keep hoping I will wake up from this nightmare and find myself back at home in my kinsman's hall with the other warriors of my house."

Kaiden slid another bottle over to him. "If you cannot go back, you must find a way to go forward, yes?"

"If I must," Aki grumbled.

"Most of us intend to go into the Pavlovan military or teach at the university or academy."

"Teach your fighting skills to those younger than you?" Aki nodded. "That is good."

"Yes and our telepathic skills." Kaiden hesitated. "We were given... extra powers. We aren't normal soldiers."

"You look normal except that your thoughts are closed off from me like they were within a shield wall."

Rolf spoke up again. "We can teach you how to do that. We can also teach you how to fight."

For the first time in a long while, Aki chuckled. "You think you can teach *me* how to fight?"

Rolf's answering smile was sweet. "I'll have you begging for your life in less than five minutes."

Aki tipped back his head and roared with laughter. "I think not, little man." He reached for Rolf only to have Kaiden step in front of him.

"Not in here. We have a training room below."

Aki finished his second ale and wiped his mouth. "Then lead on."

"ELLI, are you sure you want to teach him?" Ash asked.

She gazed up at her powerful cousin, noting the concern in his blue gaze. Her parents were dead and Ash's family were her closest living relatives.

"Why, what's wrong with the idea? I am a trained counselor. I could help him adapt."

"You are also attracted to him."

She felt herself blushing. "So what if I am? I can be professional."

"I know you can, but I'm not sure about him." Ash hesitated. "He doesn't understand our culture and he might…offend you. I don't want you to be hurt again."

"Oh, Ash, you are so sweet, but I'm over all that." Elli patted his arm. "Aki's biggest problem is his inability to shield his thoughts. Once he's mastered that he'll feel so much better, and so will everyone around him."

"But he seems to feel something for you."

She shrugged. "As you said, he doesn't know *what* he's feeling at the moment. He might react to every single Pavlovan female in the same way."

"As long as you are sure." Ash kissed her cheek. "I'm happy to arrange for you to tutor him—if he agrees."

"Thank you, Ash." She kissed him back. "Now go and do all that important stuff running the planet and I'll go and see how Aki is settling in."

She stayed where she was until Ash closed his office door and then contemplated the awesome view over the city skyline. In an exceptional family like Ash's she'd always felt like an underachiever until she'd discovered her talent for nurturing telepathic growth and counseling those learning to deal with their ever-evolving abilities.

Joining the space corps and traveling throughout Pavlovan space had helped her create a separate identity and only enhanced her teaching skills. She'd dealt with several rescued Etruscan telepaths who had barely been allowed to survive in a culture that hated their talents. Aki was a challenge she would gladly embrace because she knew she could really help him.

Sure, she was attracted to him. Who wouldn't be?

She set off down the stairs to the lower level, leaving Ash in his apartment. Her confident smile faded as she descended. Gods, she'd never felt like this about any male before in her life. Her intense feelings for Carlin seemed like pale imitations of the visceral reaction she was having to Aki. Maybe Carlin had been right to run away from her and ask the Oracle to release them from their partnership. Maybe she was too needy for any male.

That had hurt her badly—to be publicly abandoned by her First Male and left with no mate. Such a thing didn't happen often and since Carlin's abandonment her name was always recognized and pitied. She'd learned to raise her shields, behave impeccably and *never ever* show any interest in acquiring another mate. But from the first moment she'd seen

Aki's scathing magnificence, she hadn't been able to look away…

She took a deep breath and opened the door into the lower apartment. The vidscreen was still blaring, but the room appeared deserted. She paused for a second and heard a muted roar from the training center below. With a resigned smile, she went down yet another level. It hadn't taken Aki and the other Earth telepaths long to get down to basics.

The smell of sweaty male and testosterone hit her like a wave as she came into the gym. No one noticed her. They were all fixated on the battle going on between Aki and Rolf. Elli eased forward until she had a good view and almost swallowed her tongue as Aki's half-naked body came into view. He had a bluish-black tattoo that covered his right shoulder and most of his arm, and his stomach rippled with muscle as he charged at poor Rolf with an almighty roar.

Rolf stood his ground, and in a blur of motion, altered his stance and hip checked Aki, sending him sailing over his head to land with a gigantic thud on the mat. The watching soldiers cheered and clapped as Aki stayed down. Rolf sauntered over and held out his hand.

"As I said, Viking, size isn't everything."

Aki took the proffered hand and got to his feet, his blue gaze locked with Rolf's.

"I do not understand how you bested me, little man, but you have." He slapped Rolf so hard on the shoulder that he rocked on his feet.

"It wasn't really a fair contest," Rolf admitted. "You have magic in your thoughts and spells. I have magic in my body, which makes me super strong—like a berserker."

"Ah," Aki nodded. "You cannot give me this magic."

"I can teach you some of it." Rolf tapped his forehead. "The parts that come from my thoughts."

"Then I shall be glad to learn from you." Aki bowed.

"And I'm sure we'd all like to learn some of your tricks with an axe or a sword." Kaiden stepped forward. "Some of the people on this planet don't use guns or advanced technology. Understanding basic warfare techniques would be an advantage."

"I am sure that once my brother stops rutting long enough to meet you, he would be more than willing to show you our skills." Aki grinned at Kaiden. "He is a fearsome swordsman while I favor the axe."

Kaiden slung an arm around Aki's shoulders. "I think you will fit in well here. Come and eat."

As Aki turned he spotted Elli and came toward her.

"Did you see me laid low by that heathen Rolf?"

"I'm afraid I did." His ability to take his defeat with a smile had impressed her. She tried to look at his face, she really did, but rivulets of sweat were running down over his chest and abs and she wanted to lick him clean and follow the trails down lower until…

"My lady?"

She jumped as Aki moved close until she could smell his sweat, which was normally a complete turn off in a man, but somehow made *him* even more delicious. She licked her lips.

"Sorry?"

He reached forward, put a finger under her chin and gently closed her mouth. "You are staring."

"I know."

His smile was just for her. "I do not mind, but if you continue to do so, I fear my interest will become obvious to everyone."

Her gaze slid lower to his low-slung, black workout pants and the thrust of his erection tenting the fabric.

"Oh Gods," she breathed and backed away two steps. "I'm so sorry. I'm embarrassing you."

"Nay, you are making me hard." He cupped himself and ran a

thumb up the length of his cock. "It has been a long time since I've felt like this."

"When you were in the ice, were you aware of anything?" she asked.

His gaze became distant. "It was like being trapped underwater. I occasionally became aware of something, but it was all very faint until the Pavlovan eclipse."

Realizing everyone had already gone upstairs, she started toward the door. "That astrological event only happens about every four thousand years. I suppose you could say you were in the right place at the right time."

His laugh was short. "Sometimes I think it would have been kinder to have left us where we were."

She turned toward him, only to see his gaze fall over her shoulder as Kaiden's voice boomed out.

"Come on, Aki. There's food. Are you joining us, First Officer Slavin? There's plenty."

***

THE FOOD WAS good and being in the company of warriors made Einarr's continuing absence easier to bear. But Aki missed his twin. He missed their easy communication. Einarr was his only blood kin in a world where he was adrift without his solid presence at his side.

It was almost impossible for him to shut Einarr out of his head, so he'd spent the dinner feeling like he was spying on his brother fucking his woman. His cock throbbed like a toothache and refused to go down. Sitting next to Elli wasn't helping much either, her thigh was jammed against his on the bench and every time she reached for more food, her breast brushed his arm.

"Ash wanted me to ask you something,"

Aki turned to Elli, his eyebrows raised. She was slightly

flushed, her tongue peeking through her lips. He wanted her mouth on him so badly...

On his other side, Rolf gave a snort, and Aki swung around. "What is so amusing?"

"*You and your lack of shielding. You're blasting out the most filthy images.*"

"*You have no shields yourself then?*" Aki asked politely. "*Perhaps you shouldn't be peeping.*"

"*I have excellent shields, but I must confess that I'm enjoying the show.*" Rolf's gaze dropped to Aki's pants. "*If you are still hard later come and find me. I'd be more than willing to get down on my knees and suck you off.*"

Aki's cock kicked up even more and he barely suppressed a groan before turning back to Elli who had been waiting patiently for him to finish his conversation. Hopefully, her shields had protected her from Rolf's coarseness.

"Excuse my rudeness." Aki bowed. "What did you wish to ask me?"

"Ash said you need to continue your studies while you decide what you wish to do on Pavlovan."

Aki groaned. "More teachers?"

She angled her head to one side. "What if I was your teacher?"

He went still, almost too afraid to speak or even to think all the various images that offered him. "*You?*"

"Would that offend you?"

He stood and grabbed her hand. "You may tutor me in any way you wish." He managed to get her outside the door before she started to pull against him.

"What are you doing?"

"Taking you to bed." He turned her so that her back was against the wall and leaned down.

"Stop!" She slammed both her hands against his chest.

Mystified, he shut the door behind them so that they were alone in the narrow corridor.

"You do not want me?" He inhaled her scent. "I can almost taste your need on my lips. Teach me how to please you."

She let out her breath. "That's not quite what I was offering you."

He braced his hand on the wall above her head and forced himself to ignore the demands of his body—and hers—and concentrate on her words. Life had been much easier for his ancestors who could simply toss a woman over their shoulder, take her home and ravish her at will.

She smacked him on the chest. "That is so not funny. Those poor women!"

"I have never done that!" he protested. "I am an honorable man. You take my thoughts now and use them against me? Is nothing private?"

"Not until you learn to shield better. That is what I'm offering you help with. I'm a trained telepathic counselor."

"What does that mean?"

"I can show you how to build the strength of your shields and increase the power of your thoughts."

"Oh." He studied her closely and then took her hand and brought it to his lips. He liked her bravery and her willingness to stand up to him. "I will do my best to learn these things if you are willing to teach me."

"Thank you." She smiled into his eyes. "I'll give you a couple of days to settle in and then we can start your lessons."

To his dismay she pushed gently on his chest. "I have to get back to work now."

He fought down the desire to beg her to stay. He was becoming a weakling and he hated it. "You are quite certain that you do not wish to join me in my bed? I swear I will give you more pleasure than you have ever imagined existed."

She shivered. "And now you are a poet. I won't sleep with you Aki."

He kissed her nose. "You will not be sleeping, my heart—unless I have worn you out with my lovemaking. And even then I will wake you up and make you want me again."

"Oh Gods," she whispered. "This is *so* not happening to me."

Her words made no sense but her mind closed against him and he took an unwilling step back. "I do not understand."

"Which is why us getting together would not be a good idea at the moment." "We hardly know each other." She met his gaze head on. "You need to get used to being here and living with millions of telepaths."

"And then you will bed me?"

"You are way too persistent." She pushed a lock of her hair behind her ear. "I don't know, Aki. You might not feel the same about me when you're more in balance."

"I will still want you."

Her smile was sad. "It doesn't always work out that way, but I appreciate the thought."

Aki took another step back and bowed. "Then I will wish you Godspeed, and look forward to seeing you again soon."

Her gaze softened as she stood on tiptoe to kiss his cheek. "It's going to be okay, Aki. I swear it."

So his attempts to deceive her about his fear of being left alone hadn't worked. It stung his pride. There was nothing he could do about it but accept her kind offer and improve his shields.

After Elli left him, Aki returned to the main room and got himself another ale. It was difficult to remember that this new world had its own set of rules and customs that he did not yet fully understand. He wanted Elli. He was fairly certain she wanted him back, but that apparently wasn't enough. He frowned. What were the courting rituals of the Pavlovans? Did he need to seek the approval of Elli's father? Or should he speak to Ash?

Rolf nudged him in the back and Aki spun around. "What *now*?"

"She likes you."

"She is merely being kind."

Rolf shook his head. "Nope, I can feel the vibe."

Aki shoved a hand through his disordered hair. "I do not know what that means. All I know is that the females on the planet make no sense."

"I'd agree with you, seeing as I tend to prefer men."

Aki studied Rolf's features. "You have to choose *one*?"

Rolf chuckled. "Not if you believe in the idea of this Pavlovan mating trio. It tends to be two men and one woman. You get the occasional one man with two women, or all the same sex, but most triads are male heavy." Rolf shrugged. "At some point Ash said he will take us all to see the Oracle."

"And what will this seer do for you?"

"She introduces you to your fated mate. Or, if you're really lucky, both of them. That's how Esca came to be Ash's Second Male at age eighteen"

"And the Oracle is always right?"

"By all accounts, she is pretty damn good. There are only a handful of failed matings a year here, which is quite something compared to Earth."

Aki shook his head. "The women in my village were free to leave a man if they wanted, and no one cared whether you fucked another man or a woman." He hesitated. "But the new religion, the Christian one, insisted one man had to cleave to one woman. Some of our people tried to keep worshipping both Gods, but it was hard for them."

Kaiden stood up and nodded to Aki and Rolf. "I've got to go to a bloody strategy meeting in Mac's place. Will you keep an eye on Aki for me, Rolf?"

"That will be my pleasure, sir."

Aki grunted as he watched Kaiden leave. "At least I only have to put up with you watching me. The security forces followed our every move on the other planet."

"That's because you passed basic onworld training. You're no longer considered a major threat to society," Rolf said. "They're still watching all of us, but it's much less obvious and we have more freedom. We have to prove our worth, which makes sense when we could be dangerous."

"I suppose it does," Aki agreed. "No ruler wishes his kingdom to be invaded by armed mercenaries. The Saxons fought hard to keep us out of their lands until we overwhelmed them."

The other guys relocated to the seats in front of the big moving picture screen, and Aki finished his ale.

"Do you want me to show you to your room?" Rolf asked.

Aki held his stare. "That would be very good of you."

Rolf winked at him as he got up, and they walked down a hallway that had several doors leading off it. He stopped at the last door at the end of the hall and tapped in a code.

"Give me your hand."

Rolf pressed Aki's palm to the panel on the right-hand side of the door and pressed the keypad again until it blinked three times. "You're in. All you have to do is place your palm in the square just like you did then and the door will open."

"Thank you."

"Seeing as I kicked your ass, earlier, it's the least I can do."

Aki went through the door and then grabbed Rolf's black T-shirt in his fist, practically hauling him off his feet. "I am more than willing to fight with you again."

"You don't have to prove your masculinity because the lady turned you down."

Aki bared his teeth and growled, but Rolf leaned into him instead of away.

"I like you mad. And I'm always willing to be handed my ass." Rolf licked his lips. "Although I'd rather give you a better welcome to Pavlovan by offering to be the first man in four thousand years to suck your dick. I bet you've worked up quite an appetite, haven't you?"

"Why would you think that?"

"Because I saw your thoughts, remember?" Rolf said patiently. "And if I'd been frozen for thousands of years I'd be wanting to get laid pretty damn quick to make up for lost time. And seeing as the female won't have you..."

He removed Aki's fingers from his shirt and sauntered toward the bathroom, pulling the garment over his head as he went. "Come on."

Aki followed more slowly and heard the sound of water being turned on. One thing he did secretly love about his new life was the availability of hot water. After being incarcerated in ice, he had a feeling he would never be warm enough again.

By the time he reached the large shower, Rolf was naked, and Aki paused to consider the other man's muscled body. Unlike Aki, he had no visible scars, but it didn't matter. His battle experience showed in his eyes and in his warrior's stance. Aki slowly took off his shirt and Rolf grinned at him.

"Nice tat."

Aki glanced down at his arm and shoulder. The magical designs were so much a part of him that he hardly even noticed them.

"This...favor you offer me."

Rolf raised an eyebrow. "Sucking you off?"

"It does not mean that we are mated or matched as the Pavlovans would call it?"

"Nah. I don't feel like that about you, and I'm getting nothing off you. This is just for fun. Kind of a welcome-to-your-new-world thing. Did you ever do that back in your day?"

"At the festivals, yes."

"Then think of this as pure pleasure with no expectations on either side." Rolf snapped his fingers. "Take off your pants. I want to see you."

Aki obliged and Rolf fell to his knees, his tongue emerging to lick Aki's already erect cock. "Damn, you're big." Even as he murmured the words, Rolf was sucking Aki deep into his mouth.

The explosion of senses made Aki's knees wobble as Rolf brought him to a hard and brutal climax. Within minutes, he was coming down Rolf's throat, his hand fisted in his partner's thick, red hair. Was it wrong that he thought of Elli while he did it? Wished she was kneeling at his feet and struggling to accept the length of his cock?

He gulped in some air and released his rigid grip. "That was…good. I thank you."

Rolf got slowly to his feet, wiped his mouth and headed into the shower. "That was just an appetizer. Let's clean up and then if you feel like it, I can show you the rest of my repertoire."

2

"GOOD MORNING, BROTHER."

Aki turned to see Einarr entering the kitchen area. He had the smug look of a well-satisfied man and moved rather slowly toward the white box with the icy insides where food was kept. Aki had opened it accidentally once and recoiled from the coldness.

"I am surprised you can even walk," Aki grumbled.

Einarr smirked. "Frey cannot, which is why I am bringing her breakfast in bed."

"Do not pretend you know how to use the implements. Chase will be back in a minute to serve you. She does not appreciate 'Vikings rampaging through her pantry.'"

Einarr snorted and Aki raised an eyebrow. "I have not seen you for two days. The least you could do is sit down and talk to me for a few moments."

Einarr's smile faded. "What is wrong?"

"Something has to be wrong before my twin can tear himself away from his lover's arms and speak to his only living brother?"

"I am sorry. I know I am not being fair to you, but seeing Frey again…sharing her body and her mind has been the best experience of my life." He took a seat opposite Aki. "You have my permission to laugh. I never imagined I would meet a woman who consumed me as Frey does." Einarr sighed, reached across the table and took Aki's hand. "I have also been neglectful of you."

"I have managed quite well by myself. The soldiers from Earth have been most welcoming…" He thought about Rolf's talented mouth. "Most welcoming indeed."

"Good. I will make time to meet them today, I promise you."

The door opened and Chase, the woman who ran all the kitchens in Ash's large dwelling, came in and smiled at them both.

"Oh, Aki, he *does* look like you. His hair is quite different, but you both have such lovely blue eyes."

Einarr rose to his feet, strolled over to Chase and bowed. "It is a pleasure to meet you."

Chase shook his hand. Aki reckoned his brother was almost two feet taller than the diminutive cook.

"Now are you looking for something to eat for you and your young lady? What does she fancy?"

Einarr frowned. "I do not know."

Chase laughed. "Then I'll give you a bit of everything and you can surprise her." She opened one of the cupboards. "Would you like some more pancakes, Aki?"

"Yes, please." He'd been a bit suspicious when Rolf had persuaded him to try the flat brownish circles. They resembled oatcakes but they tasted remarkably like the flat patties his mother used to make. After he'd been introduced to the sticky syrup that went with them, he'd quickly decided they were very good.

Einarr strolled back over to him and swiped a piece of pancake from his stack. "This is excellent."

Aki slapped his hand. "Get your own."

"Sit down, Einarr. I won't be a minute," Chase bustled around the kitchen. "I'll make you up a tray in no time."

Einarr sat and Aki lowered his voice. "How did you know Frey was your woman?"

"It was obvious."

"In what way?"

"In all the ways that mattered. I just knew that she was mine." Einarr shrugged his wide shoulders. "I cannot really explain it."

"Do you think everyone is supposed to feel like that when they meet their mate?"

"I do not know. You should ask the Pavlovans." Einarr looked at him more closely. "Why?"

"Because I thought there was something between me and Elli. Her thoughts call to me, as does her body. She is quiet but brave and she does not allow me to intimidate her. Beneath that soft exterior, she has a warrior's heart. I have never met a woman who affects me in this way before."

"You always say that." Einarr slapped his arm. "You fall in love far too easily."

"That was in our old life," Aki insisted. "Here all is different. Here I can use my magic freely and have found a female who can accept me as I am."

"All the females here are mind thinkers, Aki. Maybe you are overreacting."

"So you feel the same way about all the Pavlovan women as you do about Frey?" Aki demanded. "She is no different to them?"

"She is my mate." Einarr growled and thumped his fist on his broad chest. "I know it here."

Aki sat back. "See? You know it. I did not think of your Frey like that for a second. I think Elli is meant to be mine."

"Then tell her."

"I tried. She insists that I do not know my own mind and is keeping away from me and out of my bed."

Einarr let out a breath. "If she truly is your mate. I suspect that whatever you feel for her will resolve itself and become clearer. If she is right and the feelings disappear, then you will certainly know it."

"I don't know what I feel or who I am anymore," Aki groused.

"Then give yourself time to find out."

"Your tray is ready, Einarr," Chase called out.

"Do you wish me to speak to Elli Slavin about this?" Einarr asked.

"You? I don't think so. But maybe your female could? They are friends."

"I'll ask her." Einarr stood and slapped Aki on the back. "I will see you later, brother."

Einarr went back to feed his woman, and Aki contemplated what lay ahead of him for the day. Exercising with his fellow warriors, learning the Pavlovan language so that he could do without the translator and maybe going out in the city.

He'd been out twice now and both times he'd hated the experience. There was nothing he could understand or relate to out there. The people were not like him, and the buildings and vehicles made him feel dizzy and small. Aki heaved a sigh.

There was no way of hiding it. He was afraid to go out into this alien world. Even looking down at it from the top of the building made him feel like emptying his innards. And the sounds of city... Not just the incessant rumble of noise that found its way even through the thick glass, but the thousands of mind talkers he couldn't escape...

"Here are your pancakes, Aki, and someone else to visit you. Good morning First Officer Slavin."

Aki looked up to see Elli standing by the door. She wore a dark blue garment that covered her from neck to waist and a short, tight skirt fitted to her body and displaying the length of her legs. Her fair hair was tied back at the nape of her neck and she wasn't smiling.

He still wanted her.

"Hey, Chase, hi Aki." She came to sit opposite him. "I wondered whether you'd like to make a start on those shielding lessons?"

If it meant he didn't have to venture down into the city he would agree to anything.

"I would like that."

"The other guys are going out so we can sit in here and work without disturbing anyone." She waved at his plate. "Finish up first. I'll get some coffee."

ELLI WANTED to sit in Aki's lap and feed him the pancakes and then maybe pour a bottle of syrup all over him and lick it off...

Yeah...

She was *so* not needy. She forced herself to get some coffee, spoke briefly to Chase before she left to prep Ash's lunch, and gave herself a severe talking to. Aki was her student. She had to remain aloof and in control around him. Only when he was fully integrated into Pavlovan society would she have the right to find out what his feelings were about being mated.

The fact that she was even using the "M" word again was a big deal. She'd decided she was done with all that after Carlin had publicly disowned her. But Aki was so... *gorgeous*. She glanced over at him and almost choked on her coffee because he was staring right back at her.

As if in a dream, she watched him pick up his empty plate and bring it over to the sink. He wore a tight black T-shirt and pants that did nothing to hide his bulging muscles. She'd never been into men who worked out before, but now she wanted to climb him like a tree.

He put his plate in the sink and turned toward her, his head angled to one side making his fair hair fall over his shoulder.

"You confuse me, Elli."

She licked her suddenly dry lips. "In… in what way?"

"You study me as if I am something you would like to devour and yet your mind remains clear."

"That's because I have good shields."

He frowned and moved closer to trace the line of her brow. "It is ironic that the one person I would like to hear my thoughts chooses not to hear me."

"As we've already discussed, you need to work on this so that you can choose to share your thoughts with whomever you *want* rather than broadcasting everything to everyone."

"You think I imagine being in bed with everyone?"

She blinked up at him.

"You think I imagine stripping the clothes from every Pavlovan and using my mouth on them?" His thumb moved lower and traced the curve of her lips. "I imagine your mouth on me, too."

She took a hasty breath to argue with him, but instead used the tip of her tongue to touch the pad of his finger.

"Elli…" He shuddered. "Please."

He pushed his thumb deeper into her mouth. She didn't stop him and sucked on him instead. With a groan, he lowered his head and replaced his thumb with his lips and tongue, taking possession of her mouth in a way that offered her no quarter.

She forgot her name, forgot that they were standing in the kitchen of Ash's apartment and simply kissed him back. He tasted of syrup and coffee and male and she wanted to drown in the rough combination of hardness and sweetness…

He picked her up, settled her on the countertop and moved between her knees. His head lowered, nuzzling her throat, biting her to hold her still as his hand crept up her inner thigh and curved over the damp mound of her panties.

"Oh, Gods…" she breathed as he slid one long thick finger beneath the silk and barely up inside her. His thumb settled over her clit, and just like that she came apart, clutching a handful of his long blond hair in her fist as she climaxed.

He lifted his head and slowly inhaled. "You want me, Elli. Do not deny it. You are slick and wet and ready for my cock."

She could only stare helplessly into his blue eyes as he licked her juices off his finger.

Behind them, someone delicately cleared his throat. She slid off the countertop and turned to face the intruder, checking to see that her skirt was all the way down.

"I apologize for interrupting, Elli, but I needed to speak to you both." Ash came further into the kitchen, his expression far too innocent for Elli's liking, although he winked at her as he went past.

Aki wiped his hand slowly across his mouth and looked dazed. She reckoned she probably looked about the same. What was wrong with her that she could forget all those years of restraint and perfect behavior and allow a man to touch her like that in public? Anyone would think she had finally found the right male for her. She pushed that traitorous thought away. Rushing into anything when she was so aroused like a naïve fool would be fatal.

"Good morrow, Ash."

"I had a message from the Oracle this morning," Ash said. "She wishes me to take you and Einarr to her Temple at Quoxor as soon as possible."

Elli sat down hard on the nearest stool. So much for putting distance between her and Aki. It seemed as if she would be separated from him regardless. That bothered her far more than it should have.

"Why?" Aki asked.

"I don't know, but in my experience, when the Oracle tells you to do something, it's usually best to comply," Ash said. He nodded at Elli. "She wishes you to accompany Aki so that you can continue your 'lessons.'"

Elli couldn't decide whether to laugh or cry.

"What about Einarr and his female?" Aki asked.

"I have already spoken to Einarr and Frey. They are coming as well. We will be leaving tomorrow." Ash nodded and headed for the door. "Carry on."

Aki sat down and slammed his hands against the table, making it rock. "I do not like being ordered around."

"You can't really argue when it's the Oracle who is doing the ordering. She can see into the future, Aki. If she wants to meet you and Einarr so urgently, she must know something important."

"Mayhap she has found a way to get us back home?"

The hope in Aki's blue eyes made Elli feel selfish for her lack of pleasure at that thought. "Who knows?"

He patted the seat next to him. "We should continue our lesson. It was becoming far more enjoyable than I had expected."

She stayed where she was and crossed her arms over her bosom so that he wouldn't notice her nipples were hard and begging for his attention.

"I didn't mean to kiss you. It's unprofessional."

"I do not understand your 'professional.'" He sighed. "I enjoyed kissing you. I want you naked and stretched out under me, Elli, but you seem determined not to believe I know my own mind."

"Perhaps when we see the Oracle she will be able to tell you whether we are… meant to be together."

He raised his head. "I know in my heart that we are meant to be together."

"It doesn't always work out like that, you know."

"Who hurt you, Elli?" He growled and half-rose out of his chair. "Tell me his name, and I will avenge your honor."

She reached over and pressed her palm to his shoulder, pushing him gently back down. "It's okay, really. I don't need my honor saved today." She hesitated. "It's just that sometimes we need time to decide how we really feel about something, or someone."

"You wish me to give you time?"

"Yes."

She wished he'd give her about five years but she suspected that wasn't going to happen. When had she become such a coward? Hemmed in by her own rules, afraid to even try and reach out to a man who obviously wanted her? There had to be a balance between what she'd always feared and what she suddenly craved.

"Then I will wait to hear what this Oracle of yours has to say." Aki smiled at her. "I am a very patient man, Elli. I have had four thousand years to hone that skill. But if the Oracle is as wise as everyone says she is, she will know you are mine and that I am determined to have you." He patted the seat next to him. "Now come and teach me how to guard my thoughts and I promise not to kiss you."

***

THE JOURNEY to the Oracle's Temple was accomplished in yet another form of a flying machine called an airplane. It skimmed through the skies at great speeds, and Aki spent most of his time looking out of the small window while below him the ground scrolled out like parchment. Seeing the tiny dwellings and roads beneath him, he imagined himself a hawk searching for his prey.

He also appreciated the silence. There were only about a dozen people on the air ship, and thanks to Elli's continuing lessons, he was able to block most of them from his mind and not project his thoughts outward. He couldn't imagine mastering the skill of obstructing every thought except his bonded mate's and his family, but Elli insisted he would soon learn.

She was sitting beside him, her head on his shoulder as she slept, her hand securely in his. Einarr and Frey had vanished into one of the cabins and hadn't reappeared yet. Aki was also relieved that he'd learned to block out at least some of Einarr's thoughts, although it also made him sad not sharing everything with his twin.

Ash was working near the front of the ship and Esca guarded the door. The evening before they'd left, Aki had met Soreya, the female who was mated to Ash and Esca. She was also a warrior and had been very kind to Aki, sharing her own struggles at adapting to Pavlovan culture. She'd given him hope that the future might not be as difficult as he'd feared.

If only he could persuade Elli to believe that his need for her was true, his world would be even better. She was trustworthy, strong and very good at understanding how hard it was for him to adapt to his new life. She reminded him of the frozen lakes of his childhood with their smooth surfaces and immense hidden depths. She allowed little to disturb her calm exterior, but she felt deeply about things and beneath the surface lurked a passionate and complex woman.

Einarr was right that in his past life Aki had chosen his bedmates with an eye to their beauty and stamina, but now he was older and wiser. He smiled to himself. Far older than he'd ever expected to be, and the things that called to him now—strength, steadiness and kindness—were encapsulated in Elli. She hid her hurts well, but he still wanted to kill anyone who had made her life difficult. Leaning closer, he inhaled her scent, willing her to wake up, take his hand and walk with him into one of the cabins…

"Stop right there, Aki. I don't want to picture anymore."

Aki recognized Esca's distinct voice in his mind and raised an eyebrow. *"I apologize. I am working hard on my shields, but the occasional thought escapes me."*

Esca beckoned to him. With a resigned sigh, Aki left Elli's side and went to sit next to the formidable warrior.

"Are you serious about her?" Esca demanded. *"Because if you aren't..."*

"Ash has already warned me off." Aki held Esca's gaze. *"But I still want her and believe she is meant to be mine."*

"She's had a bad experience with mates."

Aki frowned. *"I knew someone had hurt her. She is reluctant to believe that I could want her. She keeps telling me that I must be certain and not make a mistake. What happened to her?"*

"It's not my story to tell, but then I've never been known for my ability to hold my tongue. All I'm going to say is don't hurt her, and don't go public about how you feel about her unless you are one hundred percent certain you mean it."

Aki nodded. *"I understand."*

"If you hurt her, Ash will be upset. And nothing is allowed to upset my First Male, so I'll be coming for you and not in a good way," Esca added.

Aki frowned as he puzzled through what Esca had said, recognized it was some sort of threat and then nodded. *"I will not change my mind about how I feel about Elli Slavin, I swear it."*

"We'll see, won't we?" For once Esca looked entirely serious. *"She's awake and watching us. Don't tell her what we were discussing, okay?"*

"I will not betray your confidence." Aki rose to his feet and bowed. "Thank you for your counsel, Esca." He started making his way back toward Elli when a thousand screams tore through his mind and he rocked on his heels.

Elli shot to her feet. "What's wrong?"

"Didn't you hear that?" Aki clutched at his head. "Something is wrong, someone is dying and—"

A door slammed and Einarr emerged half-naked his sword in his hand. "What is going on?"

Aki spun around to look at Esca. "Someone is being attacked below us. Can't you hear them?" He winced as another wave of emotions swept over him. "Other voices now, they sound like your female, Esca."

"Etruscan?" Esca snapped.

"I do not know." Aki concentrated. "They want Ash… They—"

"Roberts, get this frakking plane down on the ground right now!" Esca shouted and ran toward the flight deck. "Ash —to me!"

Aki staggered as the floor dipped sharply to the right, sending him to his knees. He gathered Elli in his arms and stayed down as Esca continued to issue orders.

"Weapons fired." Robert's cool voice came over the system. "Fourth engine out. Brace for impact. We're going down into the Quoxor preserve."

Aki closed his eyes as the airship plummeted downward, engines screaming as Roberts continued to talk as though nothing was wrong. That man had ice in his very veins.

"Hold on everyone."

The impact as they hit something solid beneath them made Aki bite his tongue. He held Elli close to his heart, shielding her with his body as everything around them buckled and screamed and threatened to tear itself apart. When he finally opened his eyes, alarms were blaring and there was the smell of burning in the air.

Einarr shook his shoulder. "We have to get out. Do you have Elli safe?"

"Aye." He picked Elli up and followed Einarr out of the enormous hole ripped into the side of the ship. "Where are Esca and Ash and the rest of the crew?"

"Trying to put the fire out."

Aki gently deposited Elli under a tree next to Frey. Ash lay there as well, his eyes closed and a nasty gash dripping blood over one of his eyes.

Elli nodded at him. "Go and help them shut the plane down before it explodes. I'll locate the medical emergency kit and keep an eye on Ash and Frey."

Aki shoved a reluctant Einarr away from his mate and back toward the ship where Esca and the crew were dousing the flames with thick white clouds of frothing water.

Esca spared them both one glance. "You okay?"

"Aye."

"Is Ash conscious?"

"Not yet, but he is still breathing. What can we do?"

Esca gave him one of the heavy metal tanks. "Point this at the flames while I scout around the area."

Einarr shoved Aki aside. "I'll do this. You go with Esca." He nodded at the other man. "Aki will keep you safe. He is the best hunter I know."

"Come then," Esca said. "But no more words, just mind speak. And shield as best as you can."

From what Aki could tell, they'd landed in the middle of a large forest, flattening several trees during their descent. The air felt heavy and sticky, making it hard to breathe, and his clothes were already drenched with sweat. He and Esca made a wide circle around the crash site, but detected no immediate opposition or interest in their arrival.

"Can you still sense the voices?" Esca asked eventually.

Aki went still and then pointed to the north. *"Over there."*

"Which ones?"

"Both kinds of thoughts. But the enemy are far louder now." Aki

swallowed hard. He'd seen what a raiding party could do to a peaceful settlement. It was never good. *"Why do they want Ash?"*

"Because he's the leader of the senate."

"Like a king?"

"Kind of." Esca checked his weapon, his expression lethal. *"He is also my First Male. I will not allow him to be hurt. When I find out how the Etruscans targeted our plane despite supposedly the highest security level on the planet…. I will frakking kill someone."*

Aki nodded. *"I do not sense any of our enemies around us yet. Perhaps we should do a final circuit and then head back to the others."*

"Agreed." He slapped Aki in the shoulder. "If you hadn't picked up on those Etruscan raiders, we'd probably all be dead by now."

<hr>

EINARR CROUCHED BESIDE FREY. "The fire is out, and the alarms have been silenced."

"That's good." Elli forced a smile. "You and Aki probably saved us all."

Einarr shrugged. "That is only because we have inadequate shields and heard what you all managed to keep out." He shuddered. "I would rather not have to experience the screams of the dying. Who are these raiders?"

"They are probably Etruscans. They are *supposed* to be our allies, but they hate telepaths and think it is their solemn duty to erase us from the universe. They tried to kidnap the Oracle recently and now this…" Elli glanced over at Ash who remained unconscious. "They probably want Ash."

"Because he is a powerful mind talker?"

"Yes, and because he is the current leader of our Senate—the body that makes the laws for all Pavlovans."

"Ah." Einarr nodded. "A very important man indeed." He glanced over her shoulder. "Here come Aki and Esca now."

Esca paused to talk to Roberts and the crew, and Aki loped toward her. He'd stripped off his shirt, leaving him in just low-slung black pants and thick boots. His blond braid was coming undone, allowing his fair hair to flow over his tattooed shoulder, and he carried his heavy axe easily in one hand.

His blue gaze fastened on her. "You are well, Elli?"

"I'm fine."

He looked over at Ash and frowned. "He is still not awake?"

"I think he must have hit his head quite hard." She paused. "I can't bring him out of it."

Aki knelt by Ash's side and placed a hand on his throat. "He is still breathing, and I feel the pump of his life blood. All is not lost. Do you think we will find help out here?"

"It's hard to tell. This isn't a very populated area, and they don't like to use technology. There are two local tribes, the Neveks, who tend to keep to themselves, and the Hakron, who supply the Oracle with the majority of her bodyguards."

"Then we will find one of their villages and get you all to safety."

Esca arrived and almost pushed past Elli in his haste to get to Ash. "Why isn't he conscious yet?"

"I need to access some of the equipment from the medic station to find out exactly what's going on. Is it safe to go inside the wreckage?" Elli asked.

Esca grimaced. "The right side of the plane is smashed into the ground. There's not much left *to* find, but you can go ahead and search."

"Thanks." Elli hesitated before she rose. "Have we sent out a distress signal?"

"That happens automatically if a Senate-registered craft goes down. They'll find us eventually—although Roberts already told me that he chose one of the remotest spots in the preserve to set down so that he wouldn't take anyone out. That means our communication links are very weak."

Aki came with her to the plane and helped her get back inside. Unfortunately, Esca had been right, and there was little left of the cabin that hadn't been compressed into a sheer tangle of metal. After a careful search, she located one mediscanner and checked to see if it was working.

"Thank the Gods," she murmured as it lit up. "At least we can check everyone out and relay the information back to the nearest medical facility."

Aki held her hand as she stepped out of the wreckage and returned to the others. Some of the six-man crew had erected a temporary shelter to give some shade and were busy checking out the rest of the area for water and for any supplies they could glean from the ship.

As a test, Elli ran the scanner over Aki and saw nothing more serious than a few bruises, which he reluctantly confirmed. She also checked out Einarr. Frey had a badly sprained ankle. Roberts and the rest of the crew were also unharmed and happy to deal with their own cuts and scrapes with the supplies Elli had in the medical kit.

Esca refused to be scanned and wordlessly pointed at Ash.

Elli crouched next to her cousin, waited for the scan to complete and then touched Esca's shoulder..

"Esca, please don't panic, but the scan suggests he is bleeding internally in his brain. We should get him to a medical facility as soon as possible."

3

Esca shook off Aki's hand and shot to his feet. "Where the frakking hal am I supposed to take him, Elli? We're out in the middle of frakking nowhere!"

Aki frowned at the male. "Do not shout at Elli. She is trying to help you." He beckoned to the pilot Roberts. "Are we able to navigate our way out of this forest on foot?"

"Yes."

"Can you find the shortest route to a medical facility?"

Roberts consulted the scanner in his hand. "There's a village to the south which should be reachable within a few hours."

"That's not damn quick enough!" Esca interrupted them.

Einarr came to stand beside Aki, his presence a solid comfort as Roberts continued to speak. "As soon as we start moving toward normal levels of the communication network we can send out additional emergency signals. They'll find us quicker." Roberts glanced over at Ash. "None of us wish to see Senator Ash's life cut short, Major Esca. We will do anything necessary to ensure he survives this."

Esca let out his breath. "I know this. I... apologize. But what about the Etruscan threat?"

"That is to the north," Aki said. "Einarr and I can take two of the men and find out what is going on there. If we can stop the invaders we will do so."

Einarr nodded his agreement. "And you can take Ash and the women to safety." He frowned. "Frey cannot walk far on her ankle."

"We'll manage. We'll rig up something to carry our patients," Esca said. "Once you find the Etruscan threat, which is closer to the full security network, you can call in backup from our military and then make your way to the Temple at Quoxor."

"Agreed." Aki bowed. Despite the danger, he felt more alive and more useful than he had since he'd first opened his eyes in this hellish new world.

Esca started issuing orders while Einarr sat down beside Frey and started binding her ankle. Aki remained in the center of the clearing until Elli came to join him. He cupped her cheek.

"You will take care of Einarr's woman?"

She scowled at him. "I'd much rather come with you. I can fight, you know."

"You are a fearsome warrior." He smoothed her lower lip with his thumb. "Which is why I trust you to protect my twin's mate."

"She is my friend. I would protect her regardless." She bit her lip. "I wish I hadn't waited."

"For what, my heart?"

"To share your bed." Her eyes filled with tears. "What happens if I never see you again?"

Aki held her gaze. "I swear to you on Odin's blood that I will stay alive and that we will be reunited at the Temple. Do you believe me?"

"I'll try," she whispered. "I'm not normally like this, I don't know why I'm even crying…"

"Because you care about me, my heart," he said gently. "I am yours. Do not forget that."

She touched his face, oblivious to everything that was going on around them. "I'm scared to say the words. I don't want you thinking I'm too intense. Last time I..."

"You can never be too much for me. I want everything you have to give." He placed his finger on her lips. "I am a man of honor." He went down on one knee and kissed her hand. "I will never betray you."

He rose to his feet and took her hand again, drawing her into the shelter of one of the trees. Bending his head, he gently took her mouth until she moaned his name and kissed him back. He wanted to lift her in his arms and bring her down over his demanding cock, sealing their bargain for all time, but he couldn't do it in such a public place and with so much to lose.

"*I am yours, Elli Slavin.*" He kissed her again. "*I will be waiting for you at the Temple. I swear it.*"

"Aki?"

Esca was calling him. With an impatient sound, Aki released Elli and walked over to him.

"I need to go. I'm leaving you Roberts and Bevan. They are both enhanced super soldiers." He held Aki's gaze. "I'm trusting you and your brother to behave yourselves, okay?"

"We will do your bidding and only that." Aki nodded. "I wish you well, Esca. And I will send up many prayers to the Gods that your First Male recovers."

"Thanks." Esca saluted. "As they are a mated couple, Einarr should be able to hear Frey clearly despite the distances, so we'll be able to keep you informed of our progress."

"Aye. Take care of Frey and Elli."

"Will do." Esca signaled to the four men carrying Ash's litter. "Let's move out."

Aki stood with Einarr and watched them go. Frey looked back at his brother for a long time, and Elli had eyes only for him.

"I feel as if someone has ripped my heart in two," Einarr

growled. "I am looking forward to meeting some of these invaders and expressing my displeasure to them in person."

"Me too, brother."

Aki turned to Roberts who was busy packing up essentials for their journey. "These Etruscans. Can we kill them?"

"They are here illegally. We're supposed to round them up and hand them over to the proper authorities to be dealt with through diplomatic channels." Roberts winked. "But Major Esca said we have his full permission to destroy the bastards who dared to hurt his First Male."

Aki smiled. "Esca is a man after my own heart. What weapons do we have?"

"Not many conventional ones. This ship isn't military. But we have you and Einarr who are weapons of a different kind." He paused. "Bev and I are pretty damn lethal as well."

"You are like Rolf?"

"Way better."

"Then we shall easily overcome any assailants."

***

"Can you share the feedback you are getting from the village as we move closer?" Roberts asked Aki as they paused to drink some water.

"Feedback?" Aki frowned.

"The impressions you are getting in your mind. Just send them outward to me."

"I will do my best. These 'skills' elude me."

"It will help me pinpoint our enemies' locations more clearly so that we will be able to kill them and not the innocent villagers."

"A worthy cause."

Einarr and Bevan had gone forward to scout out the

approach to the beleaguered village, leaving Roberts and Aki behind to guard their gear and find a place to reconnoiter.

The light was fading and they were approaching what appeared to be the outskirts of a settlement. The smell of burning drifted toward them, making Aki's throat raw. They'd heard sporadically from Frey that the other party had almost reached the medical center without incident and that Ash was still alive.

Aki focused on the mass of thoughts flowing from the village and pushed them to Roberts who winced.

"That's very helpful, but I think I've got it covered now," Roberts said. "I want to be certain we take out the right people."

"What do the Etruscans look like?"

"The same as us," Roberts said flatly. "But ninety-nine percent of them aren't telepathic. You'll notice that even more now that you're used to being surrounded by telepaths. None of their males are telepathic. They have a few females who work with intrusion units."

"Like Soreya. Ash and Esca's mate."

"Exactly. This is a Hakron village so you should be able to differentiate between them and the Etruscans."

"How?"

"The Hakron tend to have green skin and they are advanced telepaths and fearsome warriors."

"That is good to know."

"I'm trying to key into a Hakron telepathic stream to warn them of our approach, but so far they are impenetrable." His smile was wry. "They don't react well to my particular brand of telepathy. They think I'm a machine."

Aki drew his sword from his shoulder scabbard and carefully checked and cleaned the blade before sharpening the three additional daggers he'd taken from the ship. His axe was always honed to perfection. A whisper of a thought brushed his mind and he looked up.

Einarr was coming back through the trees with Bevan behind him. They both looked grim as they joined Roberts and Aki.

"Half the village has been slaughtered. There are bodies everywhere. It is obvious that they cleared a space in the center of the village and set up their rockets to fire at our airship." Einarr said. "The remainder of the population are either being held captive in the great hall or have escaped."

"How many Etruscans did you see?" Aki asked.

"Two dozen maybe?" Einarr spat on the ground. "May they rot in hell."

"Do not worry, brother. If they are not true warriors then we shall not allow them the glory of a place in Valhalla even in death."

"Amen to that," Bevan muttered. "They are using the people trapped inside the hall as bait to get the others to surrender."

A high scream reached them and was abruptly cut off.

"Then the sooner we get this over with, the better. No fucking prisoners. Shoot to kill." Roberts shouldered his weapon. "We'll surround them and take them out one at a time until somebody notices and then we'll have to go in. Agreed?"

Aki nodded, as did the other two. He was not afraid anymore. For the first time since waking up in this strange future, he had a purpose and a just cause to fight for. He finally felt alive.

"Let's keep everything telepathic from now on in," Roberts moved forward. *"And shield because the Etruscans definitely have a telepath with them."*

They went into the wooded area that surrounded the settlement and began to spread out. The sounds from the village grew louder, a horrible chorus of the dead and the dying that made Aki want to kill the Etruscans with his bare hands.

A thought slid past him, and Aki's head went up just in time to see an arrow flash past his cheek and bury itself in the fabric of his shirt, pinning him to a tree. Before he could rip the arrow out, a male was on him, his dagger right against Aki's throat.

Aki let out his breath. *"Hakron?"*

The huge male who had him pinned against the tree arched away until Aki could see his face. He had eyes the color of an angry sky, hair like soot and soft green skin, most of it uncovered apart from a swathe of checked fabric gathered with a belt at his hips. There was a bow slung over his broad shoulder and a dagger tucked into his belt.

"We are friends. We come to help," Aki said.

The pressure against his neck didn't ease, and the knife tip dug deeper, releasing a thin trickle of his blood.

"You are not Pavlovan."

"I'm from Earth."

"Ah." The Hakron male slowly smiled. He had flowers and leaves braided into the left side of his hair. *"Like Ian Mac?"*

"Yes." Aki was sure he'd heard that name somewhere. *"Our plane was taken down from the sky by the Etruscans in your village."*

There was a pause, as if the male was communicating with someone, and then the dagger was drawn away from Aki's neck.

"Welcome, Human. I am Morek."

"I am Aki. There are three others here with me."

"I know." Morek smiled. *"We have you all."*

Aki allowed the Hakron to take him deeper into the forest. Despite his size, the man moved with the light grace of a hunter, meaning Aki struggled to keep up. Eventually, they reached a clearing with a set of four equally spaced boulders at the center.

Aki hesitated before entering the circle, and Morek glanced at him.

"You can sense that this is a holy place?"

"Aye." Aki put out a tentative hand to touch the stone and snatched it immediately back.

Morek studied him closely and then spoke out loud, his

accent as melodious as his movements. "The stones like you. Can you hear them?"

Aki nodded as the swell of sounds washed over him. This place was even older than he was, but it also seemed to understand and welcome him. He touched the stone again and felt the pull of emotion and countless experiences. It reminded him of the cave where he and Einarr had crossed the waterfall and been frozen in time.

"Aki."

He blinked as Morek touched his arm and the resonance of the stone seemed to flow through him and consume Morek, too. For a moment they were all one and Aki groaned as his mind was filled with so many images and feelings and…

"*Aki.*"

Morek dragged him away from the stone and held him upright against a tree. "Are you well?"

He looked into the other man's worried gaze and managed to nod. Whatever had just happened, he would never forget it. The stones knew his history and somehow that made his loneliness much easier to bear.

Morek slowly smiled at him and cupped his chin. "You are extraordinary. I knew you would be." He bent his head and kissed Aki full on the mouth and then stepped away, looking to his left. "The others are coming."

Aki remained pressed against the tree like a mindless fool still caught in the magic of the stones and the sense that Morek was somehow part of it. Was it normal for Hakron warriors to kiss other men? Not that he objected. The snap of attraction left by the stones had made him more than willing to be touched by the other man.

Einarr emerged from the trees and like Aki, halted before the stones.

"Touch them." Aki said. "They know us. They are ancient."

The male beside Einarr looked questioningly at Morek who shrugged. "I do not understand it, Ungar, but Aki is right."

Morek turned to Aki. "This man is of your family?"

"Einarr is my twin."

"As Ungar is mine." He gestured at the man with Einarr who nodded at Aki. "We are both bodyguards to the Oracle when she resides in the Temple of Quoxor. Luckily, we were on our way home for a family celebration when the Etruscans struck." He slammed his fist against his palm. "They have killed many of my people. And now they are using the young and the old as hostages to force us to lay down our weapons."

"How many of you are left out here?" Roberts and Bevan had also appeared in the clearing accompanied by one Hakron male and one female.

"Just us four."

Roberts smile was cold. "Then between us we should have no problem killing every single one of the Etruscans should we?"

Ungar's answering smile was savage. "We are still few but we will die trying."

"I've no intention of dying," Roberts replied. "All we need to do is come up with a plan and carry it out."

THEY HAD PAIRED OFF, each of them with one of the Hakron who knew the area better than they ever would. Aki was crouched beside Morek on a small rise behind the village, which gave them an excellent view of the main hall where the captives were being held. The Hakron village was comprised of simple stone and thatch structures that reminded Aki of his old home.

Between the eight of them they'd already taken out four Etruscans who had been sent to patrol the forest, leaving twenty or so of them left to deal with. The plan was to move in closer and take out the secondary guards before launching a full assault on the remaining soldiers guarding the hall entrance. The telepathic Hakron inside were well aware of what was happening and would be quick to help their rescuers if the opportunity arose.

Morek notched an arrow as one of the Etruscans wandered away from the watch fire and toward the forest. Within a second the man fell quietly into the lush foliage, an arrow straight through his throat.

"Good shooting." Aki remembered to mind talk just in time.

"Thank you. Now I will take out the man by the fire before he becomes anxious for his companion's return." Morek suited the words with his actions, and the Etruscan slumped forward like a puppet.

"I am not sure you need me here, Morek."

Morek smiled. *"Oh, I need you, Aki. Never doubt that. My brother and I knew you were coming to us years ago."*

Aki frowned. *"How could you have known that when I didn't even know I would wake up here four thousand years after my supposed death?"*

"The Oracle told us on our eighteenth birthday." Morek slung his bow over his shoulder and beckoned for Aki to follow him down the slope toward the fire. *"She is rarely wrong."*

"What exactly did she say?"

Morek grinned at him. *"Enough to convince us both to wait."* He crouched down beside the fallen Etruscan and relieved him of his weapons. *"We can speak of this later. Roberts says we are ready to move in."*

Eight more Etruscans were dead, and Roberts was somehow feeding into Aki's head a very detailed map of exactly where each Etruscan was situated compared to Aki's position. It was quite disconcerting.

Morek shook his head. *"Roberts is as strange as Ian Mac. Their thoughts are like a machine."*

"And what is Ian Mac to you?"

"He's the First Male of the Oracle's First Daughter. He came from Earth like you." Morek smiled. *"His Second, Willow, is a cousin of mine."*

"Ah, so Ian Mac is a super soldier like Kaiden and Roberts and the others."

"Aye."

Aki stopped and stepped sharply to his right, going in low and tackling the Etruscan creeping toward him before the man was able to get off a shot. He hung onto the man, bringing him to the ground and efficiently slitting his throat.

Morek's dagger flashed and another raider died with a cut-off gurgle. Aki shoved the dead body away from him and went back to Morek who was calmly cleaning his bloody blade on a large leaf.

They shared a satisfied grin and moved on.

Roberts's calm voice came into his mind. Did the male ever get angry? *"All clear so far. We're down to the last dozen. Four are at your end of the hall, Aki, four at Einarr's. The rest are inside. Take out your four targets as quietly as possible and we'll handle the rest."*

Morek touched his shoulder and they crouched down beside the stone wall. *"These men are more dangerous because they are now aware that their compatriots are not coming back. The range is too short for my arrows. We will have to kill them quickly."*

Aki nodded and took out his axe, wishing he had his old familiar shield rather than the flimsy Pavlovan thing he'd been given.

Morek winked at him. "Ready?"

"Aye."

They rose as one and ran toward the group of four soldiers. As time slowed, Aki saw the first man turn and raise his weapon. Holding his shield high, Aki lunged in a perfect arc, cutting the man off mid yelp as he sliced his blade right through his neck. Even as the body was falling, he was spinning on the balls of his feet to confront the next soldier.

His arm was jarred by the force of the bullets pumping into the shield, which to Aki's amazement held. He kicked out with his booted foot and caught the man in the knee, sending the second volley of shots in an arc that almost caught Aki on the way down. He stabbed the second man through the heart and whirled to help Morek who was rolling on the ground with another Etruscan.

A shadow behind the dueling pair made Aki look up as another soldier emerged, his weapon firing down at Morek. The soldier screamed as Aki's thrown dagger sliced through his fingers, making him drop the gun. Aki followed him down with his axe and made short work of ending the coward's pitiful existence.

He pulled the last dead Etruscan off Morek and threw him to one side. His Hakron companion lay still, his eyes closed and a bloody track across his cheek. Aki went down on his knees and felt frantically for a pulse.

Morek opened one eye. "I'm not dead."

"Thank the Gods."

"I knew I wouldn't die today."

Aki glared at him as his heart settled into a more comfortable rhythm. "You might have told me that."

Morek had the audacity to grin. "The Oracle would not have made me wait so long for you if I were to die on this, our first meeting."

The door of the hall burst open and Roberts came out. "All clear. Come and get cleaned up."

Aki cupped Morek's chin and kissed his bloodied mouth. "It seems your Oracle has a lot to answer for."

4

Morek knelt by the pyre and threw fresh flowers into the flames before finding his twin, who stood watching in the shadows of the hut. Ungar's cheeks were stained with tears, earth and blood, as were Morek's.

"For the first time in my life I feel no sorrow for those I have killed," Morek murmured. "They deserve no respect or prayers to send them on their way."

"I agree with you, brother." Ungar patted his back. "Do you wish to stay here tonight with what remains of our family?"

"I should do so. Yet my thoughts turn to the Viking." Morek grimaced. "I am ashamed of myself."

"I, too, think of Einarr." Ungar cleared his throat. "He told me he would be willing to share my bed."

"You *asked* him?"

"I've waited over ten years for this day. I was impatient to begin." Ungar drew Morek closer. "I have already spoken with the Elders. They understand that we have a duty to meet our mates. They wish something good to come out of this night and give us both permission to leave."

"You are certain of this?" Morek looked over at the inhabitants of the hut and received a nod and a smile from the oldest female.

"Go with out blessing, Morek and Ungar. We thank you for saving us tonight and wish you well with your new mates."

Morek went over to the Elders and bowed. "Thank you."

"Go in peace."

He nodded and walked with Ungar toward the Great Hall.

"Are you nervous, my twin?"

"Aye. But Einarr has already spoken with his female, and she is more than willing to accept that I might be their third."

Morek stopped walking. "Einarr has a *female*? Does Aki?"

"I don't know, brother. Perhaps you should ask him when you offer him a place in your bed tonight." Ungar rolled his eyes. "Does it matter?"

"I… never thought I'd be in a Triad with a female."

"It is the most usual kind."

"Mayhap Aki is not yet mated at all," Morek said hopefully.

"As I said. You should ask him."

"I'm not as direct as you are. You have always been my mouthpiece."

Ungar smiled at him. "On this occasion, I suspect you will have to speak up for yourself. We have waited a long time for these Vikings, Morek. We deserve the truth."

Einarr drew Aki to one end of the great hall where they could be alone.

"Frey said Ash is recovering nicely and is being transported back to the city for further treatment. Esca is going with him. She and Elli will meet us at the Temple of Quoxor as arranged."

"Good." Aki glanced around the hall where the Hakron villagers were laying out the injured on pallets on the floor. It was now nighttime. The air was heavy with sorrow, and Morek and Ungar had disappeared to help their family mourn their losses and bury the dead. The night sky was lit up by the red glow of several funeral pyres. In his thoughts, Aki added his own prayers for the dead.

"What will happen to these people?"

"The Pavlovan army is on their way to protect this place. They'll also take away the Etruscans." Einarr spat into the rushes. "They do not deserve to be honorably buried. They used modern weaponry against a peaceful village without just cause."

"I agree with you, my brother." Aki patted Einarr's tense shoulder. "When will we leave for Quoxor?"

"When Morek and Ungar are ready to travel." Einarr lowered his voice even more and spoke their own language. "Ungar fights well."

"As does Morek." Aki paused. "He kisses well, too."

Einarr's gaze met his. "Ungar wants me to share his bed tonight."

"And do you wish to do that?"

"Aye. Very much."

The simplicity of Einarr's answer made Aki want to smile.

"I asked Frey, and she told me it was all right to proceed," Einarr added.

"Morek hasn't asked me, but he did mention something about the Oracle having foretold our arrival."

"So Ungar said." Einarr nodded. "Perhaps these males are meant to be ours."

Aki slung an arm around his twin's shoulder. "All the more reason for us to reach Quoxor and meet this famous Oracle. A lot seems to hang on her word."

Even as he turned back, he noticed Ungar and Morek entering the hall. They both looked rather somber. For a moment, Aki was ashamed of the carnal nature of his thoughts.

Morek met his stare and after a last kiss on his brother's forehead, he made his way over to Aki.

"Did you see the healer?" Aki asked him.

"Not yet." Morek sighed. "There were many of my family to be laid to rest. The flow of my blood, my tears and my pain seemed a fitting way to mourn them."

Aki patted the bench beside him. "Sit. I will tend to you." He went to one of the women managing the injured and came back with a bowl of warm water, a soft cloth and some healing ointment.

Morek turned to sit with his legs facing outward and Aki stood in front of him. With gentle fingers he cleaned out the gouge on the other male's cheek and patted on some of the thick, creamy balm. He continued his ministrations, washing away the dirt and blood to expose each hurt and then tending to it as carefully as he could. Despite everything that had occurred that day, a great sense of peace descended upon him as he worked his way down Morek's muscled body.

It took him a while to realize that the calming sensations flowed effortlessly from Morek's mind and had enveloped his completely. For the first time since arriving in this foreign world, he felt whole again.

"There. That is better." Aki murmured.

Aiding Morek gave Aki his first chance to really look at the Hakron male—his gleaming green skin, long dark hair and sensuously curved lips. When Morek opened his grey eyes, and stared right back at him Aki didn't look away.

"Will you come to my bed, Viking?"

"Aye, if you want me."

After the increasing incursion of the new religions in his home village, it was refreshing to find a culture that accepted a man might desire both sexes without being considered a godless sinner. And Morek's desire for him was as straightforward as the man himself. Aki could no more have denied him than he could Elli.

Morek rose in one fluid motion. "I want you more than I want to breathe."

Aki followed the other male out of the Great Hall and down several narrow streets until they came to a small thatched hut at the very end of the row. Morek opened the door and bowed.

"We will be safe here until morning. The first scouts of the Pavlovan army are already within our boundaries and have sworn to protect us from further attack."

There was a fire built into a stone fireplace on one wall, a small table and chairs, and on the other side a large bed covered in furs and animal skins in colors Aki didn't recognize.

"My main home is at the Temple." Morek took off his cloak, wincing as he flexed his bruised shoulder. "This is where Ungar and I grew up. It is a simple place."

"It reminds me of my own home," Aki said hoarsely. "I hated the Pavlovan city. This feels more… real to me."

"You wouldn't find me in one of those cities." Morek shuddered. "I went with the Oracle once and that was enough. All that noise, all those thoughts…" He shook his head. "I begged to be allowed to stay home. There were others eager to take my place. The Oracle agreed I could carry out my duties just at the Temple."

Aki undid the clasp of the cloak one of the Hakron had lent him and laid it carefully over the chair.

"Are you hungry, Aki?"

"Nay, the women in the hall fed me while I waited for you."

Morek fetched a jug and two clay pitchers. "Then shall we just share a drink to send our dead on their way to *Harven?*"

Aki took the cup and clinked it against Morek's. "We call it Valhalla."

"And what does a Viking warrior do there?"

"He fights alongside the Gods all day and then returns to the hall at night to hear songs of his exploits sung by the bards and to enjoy a never-ending feast."

Morek smiled. "That sounds like our *Harven*. Except our warriors get to enjoy other more sensual matters as well."

"As they do in Valhalla." Aki licked his lips. "All together in a big, writhing naked pile of bodies."

"I can only offer you one body—unless you wish to join your brother and Ungar?"

"Watch my brother fuck?" Aki grinned. "No, I thank you. I've had to listen to him with his female for the last few weeks. That was quite enough."

"Have you met your other mate yet?"

Aki held his gaze. "Aye. She is not convinced I mean what I say and wishes the Oracle to confirm our mating."

"She is wise." Morek nodded. "She will have to approve of me as well so it is better if all the issues can be resolved at once."

"You think you are bonded to me and to Elli?"

Morek sank slowly to his knees. "I hope so, First Male, otherwise I have waited for you in vain." He rubbed his undamaged cheek against Aki's thigh. "I wish to prove myself worthy of you."

Beneath his leather trews, Aki's cock kicked up and Morek purred and ran his tongue down the length of Aki's straining shaft.

"Let me taste you."

"What about your injuries? You—" Aki stopped talking as Morek set his teeth over his stiff cock and reached up to untie the laces that held Aki's clothing together.

He groaned as his iron-hard shaft was freed and eagerly swallowed between Morek's demanding lips. Within seconds, his hips were rolling into the motion, thrusting himself deeper and harder into the hot, wet cavern of Morek's mouth.

"Gods..." He groaned as he started to come. Morek eased up, sucking lightly on the tip of Aki's cock until his lips were shiny and smeared with Aki's seed. He slowly stood and licked his fingers, gathering the wetness and swirling it around his tongue.

With a guttural sound Aki reached for him, but Morek avoided his grasp, one hand working the buckle at his hips, allowing his chequered plaid to fall to the ground. Still holding Aki's gaze, he brought his hand down to his dripping cock and then further down between his legs.

"Fuck me, First Male."

Aki took an unsteady step toward him and then another until he was able to push Morek down onto the pile of furs and spread his thighs wide with his knee. Aki ran his fingers down Morek's thick shaft and gently pumped his own cock, bringing them together in one of his massive fists.

"Gods…" Morek strained against his tight hold. "That's—"

Aki held his gaze. "You will not come until I give you leave. Do you understand me?"

"Yes, First Male." Morek nodded as Aki stroked the tip of his cock against the tight bud of Morek's arse. "Just fuck me. I want to feel you."

Aki contemplated the size of his cock as he managed to get a fingertip inside Morek. "You are too tight. I won't hurt you like that. I want to have you all night."

"There is…oil…" Morek waved a hand at the table beside the bed. Aki found a small clay bottle and smeared his fingers and the crown of his cock in the clear liquid.

"You have taken other men like this?" Aki asked as he managed to slide one finger deep and then another.

"Not quite like this." Morek gasped. "You are my mate." Morek's thoughts blended seamlessly with Aki's. "Do you feel that?"

"Aye, as if we were two halves of the same coin? As if we were twins? Not that I have ever wanted to fuck Einarr." Aki worked his fingers free and replaced them with his cock and felt

Morek's intense reaction shudder through his very bones. "That is…good."

He lifted Morek's hips, driving himself deeper with every thrust until his entire mind and body was focused on the building pleasure in the other man. And then there was no divide between flesh or thoughts as need blended them into one being…

Fighting alongside a fellow warrior and then fucking him hard simply because he was still alive to do so was a precious thing to Aki. He sensed it in Morek, too, the need to create something new and visceral between their two working bodies both striving for dominance. Two different blades forged from steel into one. Both knowing that with the need to be strong came the need to be held and loved. Because what were they fighting for, but to protect their loved ones?

Eventually, Aki lay on his side, his knee resting on Morek's belly and his hand tangled in his dark hair. The flames crackled and whispered and for one wonderful moment as he woke, Aki imagined he was back home…

"*What's wrong?*" Morek asked. "*What makes you sad?*"

Aki unclenched his fingers and let out a soft breath. "I am more happy here with you in this Hakron village than I ever imagined I would be again. It is hard to wake up out of your time and find that your world has gone."

"What do you mean?" Morek came up on one elbow, his black hair tickling Aki's chest.

"My brother and I were frozen in ice for four thousand years by a magic spell that was only broken when the planets aligned and finally set us free."

"That is a long time."

"Aye."

"You look well on it." Morek bent to kiss him. "And I thought Ungar and I had waited forever to meet our mates."

"It does not worry you?"

"The fact that you are from another planet and are extremely old?" Morek kissed him again. "I do not care. All I know is that you fill my heart and that if you choose to stay with me I will always be content."

"You make it sound so simple."

"It is for me."

Aki sighed. "I am adrift from everything I know and everything that I took for granted. Where does your faith in me come from? I fear I have lost all mine."

Morek's grey gaze strengthened. "You have survived against impossible odds to end up here with me. How can I *not* believe that the Oracle spoke the truth when you are present in my bed?"

"How can you be so sure of me when I am so unsure of myself?"

Morek took Aki's hand and pressed it against the smooth green skin of his chest. "Because you are here, Aki, in my heart." He moved Aki's fingers to his forehead. "And here in every thought. What more could I want?"

Aki stared up at him for a long moment as a curious sensation of warmth and belonging settled around his own heart. Perhaps Morek was right and the Gods had released him at exactly the right time for him and Einarr to be happy with their own kind. Aki trailed one finger down Morek's flat stomach to play with the stiff arch of his cock.

"How about here?"

Morek's grin widened as he rolled on top of Aki. "Most definitely there, First Male. Shall I prove it to you?"

"WELL?" Einarr moved close to Aki as the final preparations were made for their departure to Quoxor. "I have not seen you for three days."

"I have been busy."

"Busy fucking."

Aki raised an eyebrow. "You cannot talk."

"I have… enjoyed my time with Ungar." Einarr's smile was thoughtful. "He is a fine warrior. Our minds flow in harmony like the two fjords that joined together in our old village to become one. I think Frey will like him."

"I pray she does." Aki hefted his pack onto his back. "Let us hope the Oracle makes the correct prophecies and that none of us will be disappointed."

Aki watched as Morek spoke one final word to the commander of the Pavlovan military team left behind to guard the village and help them rebuild.

"Disappointed like poor Elli Slavin was you mean?" Einarr shook his head. "Frey said it was horrible for her."

Aki stopped walking. "What happened to Elli?"

"Do you not know?" Einarr took a step backward. "If Elli has not mentioned it, I probably should not—"

Aki grabbed his twin by his shirt and almost hauled him off his feet. "Tell me, *halfviti*."

Einarr sighed. "Elli was taken to the Temple on her eighteenth birthday and matched with a male called Carlin Gran at a public ceremony. He was based off-planet so Elli hardly saw him for six years. When he finally returned to Pavlovan, he asked Elli to meet him at the Temple. She thought he intended to ask the Oracle about their third. But he didn't. He publicly asked to be released from his bond because he had fallen in love with two others."

"Esca told me some of this earlier." Aki' dropped his brother and his hand clenched into a fist. "Carlin Gran is a dishonorable cur. No wonder Elli is worried about whether even the Oracle can deem us a good match."

"She probably fears being publicly humiliated again."

"I would never do that to her."

Einarr winked at him and shouldered his own pack. "Then you'd better make damned sure the Oracle doesn't announce you are bonded to another male before she mentions Elli."

"Why would the Oracle do that?"

"Because as we both know all too well, Aki, the Gods like to destroy our certainties. Have you even told Elli about Morek?"

"She told me not to contact her," Aki snapped. "She said she wanted to concentrate on bringing Frey safely back to you."

"And you obeyed her?" Einarr shook his head as though Aki was a complete fool. "Talk to her, Aki. She and Frey are safe now."

Aki gave his brother a scathing look and marched off to walk alongside Morek.

"My twin is a fool," Aki muttered.

"Mine too, but I still love him." Morek glanced at Aki. He'd braided fresh flowers into his hair and the perfume lingered as he turned his head. "What has Einarr done?"

"He's suggesting that he knows more about how to handle a woman than I do."

"He is already mated, aye?"

"Yes."

"Then he probably does know more." Morek pushed through the foliage and led the way out onto a more substantial roadway. "I have little knowledge of how a woman thinks myself and I am quite willing to admit it."

"He says I should have told Elli about you."

"You haven't?" Morek walked on in silence for a few paces. "Are you ashamed of fucking a Hakron? Some Pavlovans think the Neveks and the Hakrons are inferior primitive beings."

"Nay!" Aki grabbed hold of Morek's bicep to make him stop walking. "I am not Pavlovan. I thought I should wait until the Oracle confirms that we are all meant to be together before I went ahead and told her exactly whose bed I have been sharing."

"Why would she mind?" Morek raised his eyebrows. "Pavlovans are free to share unless the mating Triad decides against it."

Aki hesitated and then found himself looking into Morek's eyes. *"She was...discarded by a previous male in a very public way. I want to tell her in person."*

"If that is the way it must be, I understand." Morek nodded. *"If she is there when we arrive, I will keep away from you both until you give me leave to approach."*

"That is very...good of you."

"If we are to be a bonded Triad, she is my female as well. It would not pay to hurt her before I even meet her." Morek slapped him hard on the back. "Now walk faster, my friend, or we will never reach the Temple."

***

"HOW ARE YOU, MY BROTHER?" Ungar crouched down beside Morek at the fireside and warmed his hands in the flames. They'd stopped for the night and made camp. Tomorrow they would reach the Temple.

"I am well enough," Morek said, continuing to stare into the fire.

"You are enjoying fucking the Viking?"

"Aye, who would not? He is a fine male."

Ungar sat down on Morek's log, shoving him further down. "Then why are you sitting out here by yourself in the middle of the night?"

"I'm on guard."

"It's my turn." Ungar poked his twin in the ribs. "I would much rather be with Einarr right now."

"Then go to him. I will take your watch as well as mine."

There was silence as they both studied the fire.

"What troubles you, my twin?" Ungar asked again gently.

Morek sighed. "Aki has a female in his sights."

"So? You would prefer an all-male Triad?"

"I've never had a female. Not because I haven't wanted one, but because the occasion has never arisen. What if Aki's female doesn't wish to be mated to a Hakron male like me with no experience?"

Ungar wrapped his arm around Morek's shoulders. "Fucking a female is easy. *Fucking* is easy." He tapped Morek's forehead. "If the connection between your thoughts is right, everything else will fall into place."

"And you know this, how?"

"From asking Ulluiao about his mating with Ian Mac and Neeve. Talk to him yourself when you reach the Temple. I'm sure he will set your mind at rest."

"Aki hasn't told her about me," Morek confessed.

Ungar frowned. "Why not? Einarr has spoken to his mate, Frey. She is agreeable to our meeting and that we might also be fated mates."

"It is more complicated for Aki and his female. I understand his reasoning. I have agreed to wait until I can meet her before any decisions are made."

"You are a good man."

"I feel like a fool." Morek glanced behind at the open door of the tent where Aki lay sleeping. "If I go back in there I'll want to fuck."

"And Aki doesn't want you to do that either?"

"Nay, he would be more than happy to accommodate me, but I'm not sure if I could take it." He glanced at his brother. "What if things go wrong? The more I share with him, the harder it will be to let him go."

"The Oracle promised us the Vikings would come."

"Aye, she did."

"Then her prophecy that they would be our mates must also stand. We cannot doubt her or ourselves at this point. Where is your faith, brother?"

"Shaken." Morek sighed. "After what just happened to our village can it be right that my First Male turns up amidst such sorrow? Why should I be happy when so many of my family are dead?"

"Because they would *want* you to be happy. They would want to hear that the Oracle's prophecy came true and that you and I were fully mated," Ungar said fiercely. "Do not give up hope, Morek. I am convinced that everything will work out as the Oracle wished."

"I hope so." Morek managed a smile.

"Now go back to bed," Ungar commanded him. "If you truly fear your Viking will be torn away from you then enjoy him while you can."

Morek rose to his feet and contemplated his brother's words. "Thank you, my twin." He bent to kiss the top of his brother's head. "You were always the practical one."

"And you are the best fighter and the thinker." Ungar winked at him. "Just don't think too much, will you, and spoil what you have?"

5

AKI WASN'T TALKING TO HER… TO BE FAIR, SHE'D TOLD HIM TO back off so she'd only gotten what she'd asked for. And at least it proved that he'd been working on his shields and hadn't been broadcasting his thoughts to everyone… Or maybe he still was and he had just managed to learn to block *her* out.

That would be just her luck.

"Elli, are you even listening to me?"

She turned to see Frey staring at her from the couch opposite her seat. Frey's ankle was much better, but she was still using a cane to walk. The medical facilities available in the Quoxor preserve were fairly basic. She'd refused to go back to the city with Ash because she didn't want to be apart from Einarr.

"Sorry, what?"

They were in the guest quarters of the very grand Temple at Quoxor awaiting the arrival of Einarr and Aki. The last time she'd been at the Temple her First Male had chosen to publicly announce his desire to uncouple with her. It was no wonder that she was still somewhat on edge.

What if Aki had realized he'd been fooling himself and didn't have a bond with her? What if—

"Elli, you are really starting to worry me," Frey said. "When Aki arrives and meets the Oracle everything's going to be sorted out."

"He's not talking to me."

"You told him to leave you alone until he reached the Temple and met the Oracle."

"Einarr's talking to you."

Frey gave her a smug smile. "But Einarr and I know we are fated and mated. He thinks he might have found our third."

"Where?"

"In the Hakron village they rescued from the Etruscans."

"Maybe that's why Aki isn't talking to me." Elli put her hand to her mouth. "Maybe he's met a nice Hakron couple and realized he doesn't need me anymore."

"Elli." Frey gave her a look. "It isn't like you to be so dramatic."

"It's this place." Elli shuddered. "It gives me bad memories."

"Well you'll be out of here soon enough." Frey grinned. "Einarr's just arrived."

The door opened and Einarr came in and went straight to Frey. He knelt down before her and kissed her hand. "My Female."

"Oh, Einarr…" Frey wrapped her arms around his neck and he lifted her high. Within seconds they were disappearing down the corridor into one of the bedrooms.

"Elli Slavin."

Elli tore her gaze away from Einarr's retreating form and turned to find Aki had come through the door. She kept her shields high, and her smile painted on.

"Aki."

He halted a few paces in front of her, his smile dying. "Am I not welcome here?"

She took a shaky breath. "You are very welcome. I just wondered if there was anything you wanted to tell me about—like whether you have realized I'm not the one for you. It's okay. Just tell me the truth—I can handle it."

She kept babbling on and his face relaxed. He crouched beside her chair.

"Elli, I missed you so very much."

His simple words did something to her insides, and she smiled like a fool. "That's good."

"Did you miss me?"

She nodded and he took her hand. "I am glad." He kissed her fingers and then the inner curve of her elbow. "May I kiss you?"

"I thought you were—" She gasped as he placed his hand firmly on the back of her neck, drawing her face down to meet his. His mouth softened over hers and the subtle touch of his tongue made her open to him. For the first time since Carlin had abandoned her, she allowed herself to fall into a kiss and let it consume her.

She clutched at Aki's massive bicep and held on, her nails digging into his skin as he continued to kiss her senseless.

"You smell like the forest."

"I could hardly smell of anything else, my heart, I've been walking through it for days."

He angled his head, tasting her in a different way. Her breasts were now crushed against his chest and her nipples were two hard points of need. He pressed closer and she opened her thighs, letting him settle in between them. They both groaned as his stiff cock pressed against her belly. She was already wet for him, the scent of her arousal drifting up to mingle with his more earthy tones.

"I want you," he said the words out loud against her lips.

"I noticed that." She touched his chest and slowly trailed her finger down until it reached the huge bulge in his leather pants.

His breath hitched as she gently scratched her nail against the soft fabric.

He covered her hand with his own. "I also know that if you wish to wait until we come before the Oracle, I will abide by your decision."

She went still. Did she want to wait? Even if he wasn't her one true mate, could she just enjoy one night with him? His shaft kicked up against her fingertips, and the desire to see him and touch him overwhelmed her.

"I want you."

He nodded. "I was told that a Pavlovan may take any lover that pleases them unless their bonded mate disagrees. Is that true?"

"Yes."

"Then will you take me?" He rolled his hips, pushing his cock hard against her hand, and her knees went to jelly.

"Yes, but I want you to know that it doesn't have to mean that we're fated mates or anything. You don't have to make any promises, and I—" She gasped as he swept her off her feet and over his shoulder.

"Which is your bedchamber, Elli?"

"The first on the left." She might not enjoy being tossed over his shoulder, but it certainly gave her a fine view of his ass. She grabbed the back of his belt and hung on.

To her surprise, he kicked the door shut with his heel, placed her gently on the bed and then simply stared down at her before falling to his knees.

"You are beautiful, Elli."

She could only smile foolishly down at him.

"You make me forget my words and think only about the pleasures of the flesh."

"That's okay," she managed to croak.

"But there are matters to discuss..."

She sat bolt upright. "No. There aren't. I don't want to

discuss anything about the Oracle, or our matches, or let anything come between us at this point."

Confusion flooded his face. "But I wish to be honest with you."

"You can be as honest as you like when we are in front of the Oracle. I don't even care if you repudiate me. It wouldn't be the first time."

"I would never do that to you. But the Hakron I spoke with suggested it would be better for us all if I made sure that you did not object to—"

She held his worried blue gaze. "Aki, did you have sex with someone in the Hakron village?"

"Aye, I did."

"Then that's okay."

He frowned. "But what if the Oracle—"

"Can we just leave all that outside this door? Can we just have sex without it having to get so *serious?*"

"But you are a serious person, Elli. I am not toying with your affections. I would not wish to do that to anyone on your planet," Aki protested. "And Ash and Esca would kill me."

She slowly pulled her top over her head and took off her bra. His words stuttered to a stop, and his gaze fell on her naked breasts.

"I cannot argue with you when you are undressing, Elli Slavin."

"Then perhaps you'd better stop arguing," she said sweetly.

His hands went to his belt and he unbuckled it and removed his axe. He unlaced his shirt, his gaze fixed on her. She shimmied out of her pants and sat cross-legged on the bed as he removed various weapons from all over his body. She could see new scars on his torso from his recent fight to save the Hakron village. She wanted to kiss every single one of them better.

"You may do that later," Aki murmured. "Come here."

He went back on his knees and drew her close to the edge of

the bed, his hands on her hips, spreading her legs wide with his massive shoulders. Elli tensed as he let out a warm breath over her most intimate parts and then inhaled.

"You smell like home."

He bent his head, and the three blond braids at his temple brushed her inner thigh. She was so aware of him that the first gentle lick of his tongue against her clit made her jump. One of his big hands settled over her hip, holding her exactly where he wanted her to be.

"Mmm…"

He continued his careful exploration, spreading her with his tongue, learning her until she was pushing upward, demanding more. He laughed against her flesh.

"Patience, my heart. I've waited four thousand years to taste paradise. I intend to enjoy every second of it."

He continued to torment and lick her and then introduced one thick finger, rubbing up and over her clit and then lower to dip inside her in an unending circle of heightening need.

She reached down and grabbed his forearm and dug her nails in deep.

"Please."

"What do you want?"

"More," she whispered.

He eased back and watched the slow penetration and retreat of the tip of his finger until she was biting down on her lip and writhing up against him.

"I'm big," he murmured. "I want you to take all of me."

"How big?"

He smiled at her and climbed onto the bed, lifting her higher against the pillows and kneeling between her thighs. "Touch me."

He took her unresisting hand and placed it over the huge bulge of his cock that pressed against the leather of his pants. He rolled his hips against her fingers and groaned. "Unlace me."

Even as she attempted to unlace his pants, his fingers continued to play with her slick, hot folds, and his thumb rubbed a steady circle against her clit. Her climax hit her unexpectedly, and she bucked against his thrusting fingers.

"Ah…" He sighed as she finally shoved down his pants and released him in all his glory. Gods, he was an impressive and somewhat intimidating sight. His cock not only long, but thick and wide as well. She wrapped her fingers around him and they barely met.

Her whole body went molten and soft at the thought of taking him inside of her. Leaning forward, she licked at the pearly wetness gathering at the tip of his crown. He growled as she sipped at him and then gently pushed her back onto the bed. She licked her lips as he stared down at her.

"Nice."

"You can taste me all you want later, my lady. But now I want to be inside you." He stroked his shaft, bringing it away from the muscled wall of his abs. "Do you want me?"

She nodded and held out her arms to him. With a soft prayer, he shed the rest of his clothes and settled over her, his knees spreading her thighs wide as he brought the crown of his cock down to rub against her already swollen clit.

"You are my true love," he murmured. "I want you more than anything in this world."

The thick head of his cock nudged against her and pressed inward back and forth in an inviting dance that begged her to ram her heels into his perfect ass and drive him home deep within her. But Gods, he was huge…

"Is all well with you, my Female?"

She opened her eyes and stared into his fathomless blue gaze. "You're big."

"Aye. I will give you much pleasure."

"And I haven't really… done this completely before."

He went still, his whole body quivering over hers, his hands braced holding him away from her. Only the throbbing head of his cock remained notched against her sex.

"You are a maiden?" Elli nodded and then almost whimpered as he drew back. "Then this will not do."

"But I *want* it to do."

His smile was ragged. "You need more time to accept me."

She grabbed hold of his massive bicep. "You are going to continue, aren't you?'

"Aye. If you still wish me to. We will take it more carefully. Are you certain that you don't wish to discuss our mating further?" He frowned. "I am honored that you have chosen me as the first male to share your bed."

"I want you. I never had sex with Carlin because we never actually lived together as mates. I waited almost ten years for him to come back to me."

"And have never wanted anyone else since?"

"I was too ashamed."

"Of what, my heart?" He cupped her chin, his blue gaze intent.

"That I wasn't good enough, that Carlin had rejected me for a reason," she whispered. "He said I was too intense—that he had to get away from me."

His scowl was ferocious. "Carlin was a fool. But at this moment, I am glad that he was a fool because he did not deserve you."

He bent and kissed her slow and sweet, reigniting all the feelings she'd feared she'd left behind during her incomplete mating.

"Now, where were we?" he whispered as he thrust his tongue into her mouth in a slow, languorous rhythm. "I want you very badly, Elli. I want to make you so wet and eager that you won't even feel my cock penetrate you for the first time."

"I doubt that."

He chuckled against her throat. "Aye, I am big, and I want to feel you coming hard around every inch of my flesh. Do you think you would like that? My cock buried deep in you as you come and keep coming for as long as I can manage to stay hard?" He bit her. "And I can stay hard for a very long time."

His fingers played gently with her clit, rubbing her wetness in circles as his big, callused finger eased deeper inside her, copying the subtle thrusting motion of his tongue. She forgot how to breathe, her body following his lead and moving with him as if they had one single purpose.

"That's nice, my heart." He eased a second finger in alongside the first and she took it easily. "If you take my cock like that, I will be in heaven indeed."

She took a strangled breath as he widened the motion of his fingers and added a third, the wet sounds of her need loud against the pounding of her heart and his soft murmurs of encouragement.

"I didn't think you would be so careful with me," she admitted.

"When you grow used to me, I will sometimes be a little more direct." He groaned. "I will fuck you as hard and as often as you like. I swear it."

At his darkly uttered promise, her body opened to him even more and he planted his thumb on her clit, making her climax and grip his thrusting fingers.

"Please."

"Aye, I cannot wait any longer. I need to be inside you." He growled and replaced his fingers with the thick crown of his hot, wet cock. *"Please take me."*

Elli held his gaze as he carefully pushed inside her. Gods, he was still so *big*.

He smiled down at her. *"Take more."* He rocked his hips very gently and another inch of him disappeared inside her. *"I want you. I want to fill you up, make you come and scream my name. I want you to forget that Carlin ever existed."*

"I think I already have."

She opened her mind to him, and his thoughts touched hers as intimately and carefully as his body. His whole focus was on her and her pleasure. Seeing that—feeling that made her open her body to him even more.

"Elli," he sighed her name and surged forward. *"By Odin, you make me so hard I cannot imagine ever wanting to come out of you."*

She let out another breath as he continued to play with her clit, making her eager to take more of him than she had dreamed possible. Gods. He was pushing deeper. She whimpered and angled her hips to allow him more room, gasped as he continued to fill her.

Another climax shuddered through her and, with a soft sound, Aki slid even further in, holding himself still as she writhed and pulsed around the hard steel of his thick length.

"Do you like it, my lady?" Aki murmured. "Being impaled on my cock? Your body spread beneath me? " He rocked his hips, sending thousands of pulses along her nerve endings like fireworks.

"Gods yes." Spoken words were beyond her now. All she had were feelings that could only be expressed mind to mind.

"Then you will like this even more." He placed his hands under her knees, widening her and raising her for the now steady thrust of his cock. Each motion brought him almost out of her and then back in again.

She grabbed hold of every piece of him that she could, desperately needing something solid to cling to as he brought her to peak after peak of pleasure. She invaded his mind, sharing her pleasure, taking his delight in her and using it to heal parts of her that she hadn't even realized still hurt.

"You are my heart," he whispered as he slowly fucked her. *"You are my female. I will never let you go, even if the Oracle denies our union."*

"Oh Gods," she whimpered as another climax crashed over

her, turning her thoughts molten and blending them with her lover's like freshly forged steel. He gathered her even closer, lifting her into his hands and pistoning in and out until he roared her name and came hot and deep inside her.

With a hoarse sound, he rolled onto his back, bringing Elli to lie on top of him. She rubbed her cheek against his muscled chest and let him hold her as a curious sense of peace flooded through her mind and soul. This was right. She didn't care what the Oracle said, either.

Aki chuckled and smoothed her hair away from her face. "That's my girl. We shall defy the Oracle together if necessary."

"I hope it isn't necessary." She kissed his warm skin. "I want to get it right this time."

"The blessing of one's Gods is never to be sneered at, Elli Slavin. I understand."

He kissed her again and she thought they might have dozed. The next thing she knew, he was picking her up as if she weighed nothing and walking her to the bathroom. Still holding her, he mounted the steps into the large bath and then sunk down in the hot, perfumed water with her still on his lap.

"You will be sore," he murmured. "This will help."

She allowed him to wash her, wrap her in a thick towel and take her back to bed. Before she'd even hit the pillow, she was fast asleep and still smiling.

AKI FOUND some clothes laid out in the room beside the bedroom where Elli slept and pulled them on. The light, white garments were far more suitable for the heat and stickiness of the Temple surroundings. He was smiling as he dressed, aware of each ache and tug of his muscles from his lovemaking with Elli and the sense that with her, and with Morek, he truly had the beginnings of a new life in his strange new world...

Even though Elli was sleeping, he could still sense her in his mind just as he could Morek. It was quite extraordinary.

There was a knock on the door to Elli's chamber and Einarr appeared.

"Are you well, brother?"

"Aye." Aki grinned at his twin. "I believe I need to speak to the Oracle with all haste."

"She's already said she will meet with us tomorrow morning," Einarr confirmed. "Now come and eat. I've seen Ungar. He said to tell you that Morek is in his usual quarters in the bodyguards' complex."

"Good."

Aki stretched and followed his brother out into the main hall where Frey and Ungar were sitting opposite each other at the table. From what he could see, they appeared to be getting on rather well.

Realizing he was ravenous, Aki helped himself to the various foodstuffs on the table. He couldn't recognize most of them, but he'd already learned that there were enough similarities with the food he'd eaten in his own time to partake of a decent meal.

After a while he began to feel as if his company was unnecessary as the other three drew closer together. Clearing his throat, he stood up and bowed.

"I believe I will go for a stroll before I sleep." He turned to Frey. "If Elli awakens, will you tell her I'll be back shortly?"

"Not too shortly," Einarr murmured with a direct look at Aki. "We have a lot to… discuss here."

"I can see that." Aki winked. "I will make sure to announce my return in the loudest tones possible."

"We would appreciate that, my brother." Einarr bowed.

Aki set off from the guest quarters, making his way up to the main Temple complex, which was relatively quiet in the evening. One of the Hakron guards he'd traveled with saw him and called him over.

"Aki, are you looking for Morek? He is on duty until moonrise."

"I was just taking a look around the Temple. It is an impressive place."

"Aye. It is ancient. The first worshippers came to this sacred spring over five thousand years ago."

"That is impressive." Aki nodded gravely. "Can I visit the spring and leave an offering to your Gods?"

"If you intend to show your face before the Oracle tomorrow, I would highly recommend it." He pointed at a stairway running down the side of the highly polished Temple wall. "Follow these steps down as far as they will go. You will find yourself at the source of the spring."

"Thank you." Aki bowed. He had a desire to pray and where better than a place where people had worshipped for thousands of years? It did not matter whether they were the Gods of his Valhalla. They still might listen to his prayers and accept his offerings.

He went down the spiral staircase, watching his footing carefully on the narrow turns until he was dizzy. He finally reached the bottom and stepped away from the stairwell and onto a white, chalky surface that crunched underfoot. As he stood there, a beam of moonlight struck the ground, awakening a thousand small ripples of light within the sand.

Aki slowly let out his breath. The place wasn't large. Water lapped at the small crystal beach and disappeared within the mouth of a cave on the opposite wall. Looking up, Aki's gaze followed the towering lines of the front of the cave. The rock was twisted like frosted branches and formed an altar festooned with thousands of scraps of fabric and metal and other precious objects that swayed gently in the breeze.

He stood back and watched as the only other person present knelt down on the waters edge, splashed his face and murmured a prayer before sending his little trinket floating out into the spring. The current took the offering, drawing it back toward the entrance of the cave. The man watched until the trinket disappeared over the edge and then stood up and bowed.

His expression when he turned to Aki was full of hope, and he smiled as he went past. "May the Gods favor you, too, sir."

"Thank you." Aki bowed.

After a while, he knelt at the edge of the water and dipped his fingers into the stream, hissing at the unexpected coldness in such a warm place. He considered what he wished to say. His world was gone. He had to accept that. There seemed no point in asking to be returned to it. Perhaps he should simply pray for those he had left behind and give thanks for his new life and the chance to live again?

"Aye," he said softly as he formed the prayer in his heart and mind. Even as he finished composing it, he fumbled in his pocket for the bead of amber he'd had since he was a small lad. There was an insect caught within the depths of the stone, forever trapped. Rather like he had been in the ice.

But now he was free…

If he allowed himself to be.

He closed his eyes and set the amber bead on the surface of the water, repeating his prayer as the offering was taken further and further away from him. Within moments he caught a last glint from the amber before it disappeared down the back of the cave.

Aki lowered his head as a curious sense of peace came over him, followed by the sharp hint of tears.

"You did the right thing, Viking."

He turned his head to see a woman sitting against the wall. He couldn't guess her age, but she was beautiful and dressed in the white garb of a Temple priestess. She patted the space beside her and Aki immediately obeyed. He leaned back against the wall and surveyed the small grotto with its deep sense of serenity and time. A serenity that also seemed to emanate from the woman sitting beside him.

"Do you think your prayer will be answered?" she asked.

"I hope so," he sighed. "I tried not to demand things but rather pray for those I have left behind and for the strength to cope with this new existence."

"Not many people get the chance to live again, Viking."

"I know that. At first, I thought it meant my brother and I were still cursed by our Gods, but now I am not so sure."

"What changed your mind?"

He shrugged. "Finding out that even in such a different place out in the starry sky, there are still people who love, laugh and bleed just like they do in my world."

Her laugh was low. "That is a good lesson to learn. You have come far in many ways, Aki."

"I suppose I have." Aki considered the moonlight that was now brightening the sacred grove. "Tomorrow I will meet with your Oracle and find out if she is as great a seer as everyone says she is."

"I believe she is considered very competent."

"Well with all due respect, my lady, seeing as you serve her, you would say that."

"I also happen to believe it."

Aki touched her hand. "I meant no offense."

"And what if she tells you that she knows of a way for you to return home?"

He went still. "I am not sure if I would want to go back. Four thousand years of being alone has changed me."

"But what of your family?"

He slowly exhaled. "I will always miss them and pray for them, but I suspect they would know I was not the same man anymore."

She nodded. "That is very true."

"And I have Einarr here with me and the possibility of a new life serving your Oracle and two people who love me."

"Also true."

Aki frowned. "I just hope the Oracle understands that Elli and I are meant to be together."

"And the Hakron warrior?"

He gave her a swift searching glance. "You know of this matter? You must be in the Oracle's confidence."

"I would like to think so." She paused. "So what if she doesn't proclaim that you are now mated to your two choices?"

"How can she not?" Aki thumped his chest with his fist over his heart. "I know these things are meant to be in my very marrow."

The woman rose gracefully to her feet. "Then let's hope you are right."

Aki stood and took her hand. "Will you offer the Oracle your counsel on this matter for me, my lady? Will you tell her that I will be loyal to Elli and Morek for the rest of my days and will live with them in her service?"

She met his gaze and he couldn't look away as the power of her mind sifted through his as if he had no shields at all.

"I will consider your request."

For some reason, Aki found himself falling to his knees and kissing her hand. By the time he looked up, she was gone and Morek stood at the bottom of the stairs smiling at him.

"Were you looking for me?"

He wore the more formal robes of the Oracle's bodyguard, which consisted of a silk-like garment belted at the hips. It came over one shoulder and was fastened with a bejeweled pin at the waist, leaving one half of his chest bare. Morek's dark hair was also tamed and braided in one thick plait down his back.

"I was speaking to one of the Oracle's handmaidens," Aki said. "She might ask the Oracle to favor us tomorrow."

"That is good. Did you pray?" Morek held out his hand and helped Aki rise. He had his spear but his arrows were absent.

"Aye."

Morek smiled into his eyes. "That is also good. Did the goddess of the spring accept your offering?"

Aki pointed toward the cave. "It disappeared down there, so I suppose that means it was accepted."

"It does." Morek took a moment to bow in the direction of the cave. "May the Oracle find favor with our wishes and desires tomorrow."

They turned together and made the journey back up the stairs. By mutual consent, Aki followed Morek toward his lodgings, which were far simpler than the rooms Aki currently inhabited and shared by many guards. Morek, at least, had a room to himself.

"Have you seen Ungar?" Morek asked.

"Aye." Aki smiled at the other man. "He was with my brother and his female."

"That explains why he isn't responding to me. Thank the Gods Ungar has excellent shields."

"They seemed to be getting on very well."

Morek nodded. "I am pleased for him. He deserves to be happy. I hope he is mated tomorrow." He sat down on his narrow bed. "And you? Was your female pleased to see you?"

"Aye. She… accepted me."

"I am very pleased for you, Viking." There was something about the way Morek's mind flowed into Aki's that soothed and comforted him without even seeming to try.

"I tried to tell her about you, but she was too afraid to 'complicate things'." Aki rubbed his chin. "I am not sure what that means, but I decided not to argue with her. All will be sorted out by the Oracle tomorrow, anyway."

"Do you think Elli will accept me?" Morek asked slowly.

"I cannot see why not. You are an honorable and beautiful male."

Morek unpinned the elaborate broach on his shoulder and the silk fell away to reveal the rest of his chest. His skin gleamed green. Aki paused to admire the sheen of his muscles as he undressed. Morek unbuckled his belt and allowed the rest of the fabric to fall to the floor. He bent to gather it up and folded it into a square, giving Aki an excellent view of the long, supple line of his spine and his tight arse.

"Come here," Aki said.

Morek turned to him, his expression quizzical. "I thought we had decided to wait until tomorrow?"

"We have." He crooked his finger. "Come here and kneel at my feet."

Morek carefully placed the silk in his cupboard and then walked over with his usual grace and dropped to his knees in front of Aki.

"What can I do for you, my Viking?"

Aki reached for the silk tie that held the end of Morek's braid and eased it free. Using his fingers he carefully combed through Morek's long hair until it lay around his shoulders.

"This is how I picture you," Aki murmured. "Wild and beautiful and ready to kill."

Morek's mouth twitched. "And bloodied?"

"Aye—that too." Aki brushed his finger over Morek's full lower lip. "But only so that we can tend to each other's hurts afterward." He framed Morek's face with his hands. "You bring me peace."

"That is good." Morek didn't look away from Aki's gaze. "As you make sense of everything that I am."

"I look forward to fighting alongside you." Aki paused. "Do you think the Oracle could find a place for me here? I do not wish to return to the city."

"But what about your Female? *Our* Female?"

Aki went still. "I haven't asked her. I will endure that place if I must but…" He shook his head. "I fear I will not thrive there."

"It is not where I would choose to live either, but perhaps if we are together and it is what our Female requires, we shall be content." Morek turned his face and kissed Aki's palm. "You should go."

"I should." Aki reluctantly released Morek and waited until he stood, which brought Morek's hard cock right to his eye level. He gave a regretful sigh. "I wish I had time to bed you properly and thoroughly."

Morek palmed his cock, releasing a thin trail of pre-cum along the length. "I will think of you while I take care of myself."

"You will not share this with another?"

Morek brought his wet fingers to Aki's mouth and rubbed them against his lips. "I am yours now. I will not fuck anyone without permission from my mates."

Aki sucked Morek's fingers clean, making the other man groan. "Good. Until tomorrow, then."

He didn't dare touch Morek again or he'd be pushing him down onto the bed and rolling with him in the covers.

"Tomorrow." Morek moved out of his way. "Sleep well, First Male."

Aki glanced down at his aching cock. "I suspect I will sleep as well as you do."

Morek's laughter followed him out of the door and back to the guest quarters. Elli was still sleeping. Einarr and his guests had disappeared and Aki barely managed to crawl into bed before he too was fast asleep.

6

———

THE CLOTHES LAID OUT FOR AKI AND EINARR WERE MORE elaborate this time and of similar fabric to the ones the Oracle's bodyguard wore. The silky white robes were long and tied at the waist with a wide sash. They helped each other get dressed and combed and braided their long hair as if they were going into battle. A servant brought them goblets of wine, which was the only sustenance offered to them. It appeared meeting the Oracle involved several rituals, but they were both comfortable with that.

There was no sign of Frey or Elli. Einarr told Aki that the females were being cared for by the Oracle's own handmaidens and would meet them at the ceremony. Aki hoped that was true. He'd had an absurd dream that Elli's fears about the Oracle had come true and he'd been mated with a strange blue plant.

Even as they walked through the pink rays of the dawn's early light, Aki carried with him a sense of unease. At the door to the inner sanctum of the Oracle, a group of people favored with an individual audience had already gathered. There were several parents with a young adult and many couples who seemed to be seeking their third. The atmosphere was taut with suppressed excitement marred with a hint of awe.

Aki saw Ungar and Morek standing in front of a large golden door, their spears crossed in front of it. Neither man made eye contact. There was still no sign of Elli or Frey.

Suddenly, a young woman with a tall headdress stepped forward and solemnly banged the gong hanging by the door three times. The massive doors opened and after Ungar and Morek stepped in behind her, the crowd was allowed to progress in to the inner sanctum.

"Is that the Oracle?" Aki murmured to Einarr.

"No, I believe that is Neeve, the Oracle's First Daughter. She is mated to Ungar and Morek's cousin Willow, and one of the Earth super soldiers, Ian Mac."

Aki studied the tall, gracious woman. She reminded him of someone he had met before but he couldn't remember whom.

"Neeve met Ian Mac on Earth and brought him and the other soldiers back to Pavlovan with her. She saved their lives."

"She has been on our world?" Aki marveled at all the connections that fate had allowed.

"Aye." Einarr steered Aki toward the back of the row of benches. "Ungar said we would be near the end of the ceremony. The presentation of the young adults always goes first."

Aki sighed and resigned himself to a long wait, aware of his inner tension as if he should be ready to fight a battle but unsure why. Was he picking up Elli's uncertainty? He hoped not.

The First Daughter raised her hands. "While we mourn the innocent Hakron lives taken by the Etruscans in Quoxor Province, we must still maintain our traditions. Nothing should stand in the way of our religion or our faith. To not celebrate would make us seem afraid. We ask that all who are mated here today make an offering to the Gods in the name of the Hakron dead and honor them."

There was a light touch on Aki's shoulder and he looked around to see Morek behind him.

"What is wrong, Viking?" Morek asked. *"I have seen Elli Slavin. She is beautiful."*

"She's here?"

"Aye." Morek frowned. *"You doubt her?"*

"Nay, I just feel that something isn't right."

Morek patted his shoulder. *"I hope not. We've had enough excitement at this Temple in the last year to last us several lifetimes."*

"So Ungar told us. He said that Ian Mac is reorganizing the security. Perhaps there will be an opportunity for me here after all."

"You should speak to Ian Mac when he returns next week. You will like him."

Ungar cleared his throat and glanced meaningfully at his twin. "It is almost time. We should progress to the front of the hall."

Aki stood and slowly followed his brother down to the bottom of the steps leading up to the dais where the Oracle sat on her throne surrounded by her priestesses and handmaidens. He hadn't looked directly at her yet. There was something about the power shimmering around her and from within her that demanded respect.

"Frey," Einarr breathed his female's name like a prayer.

Aki hardly dare look to see if Elli Slavin was there as well. Only Einarr's pointed nudge made him raise his head.

She was there.

Joy expanded in his chest, and Morek patted his back. *"See? All is well."*

She smiled at him a little tremulously, but it was enough. His gaze took in the simple white one-shouldered gown she wore and the wreath of flowers in her unbound hair. She looked beautiful, and she was his.

"Einarr Bloodaxe," the Oracle's daughter called. "Please ascend the stairs."

Einarr's face paled as he started up the steps and came down on his knees in front of the Oracle who laid her hand on the top of his head.

"You have traveled far, Einarr, and have found your new home."

The Oracle's voice chimed sweetly, but held undercurrents of power that resonated throughout the large audience chamber.

"Aye, my lady."

"Do you wish to accept your mates?" The Oracle gestured at Frey and at Ungar who also mounted the stairs and knelt at her feet. She touched their heads as well and then rose from her throne, holding both of her hands palm down over the three of them.

"With the power of the Gods within me, I bind you three to each other for all time. If this is not your wish, speak now or forever hold your peace."

Aki's breath hissed out as the blast of power echoed from Einarr's mind to his. For a moment, he could actually sense the Oracle's ability to bind a mated Triad's thoughts into one three-stranded braid.

When Aki opened his eyes, the three were holding hands and the Oracle was bidding them rise and kissing each of them. He took a deep breath and braced himself for what was to come. For some reason, the climb up to the Oracle's throne now looked very arduous indeed. He risked a glance into her face as he approached and realized, with a jolt, that she was the female he had spoken to at the sacred spring the previous night.

She winked at him.

Aki had a sudden sense that everything was going to be all right.

"Elli Slavin?"

Elli started as her name was announced and walked over to the Oracle's throne. She went down on her knees and bowed her head. Her heart thumped so hard she was sure everyone could hear it and she feared she might pass out.

"Aki Bloodaxe and Morek of Hakron?"

Elli froze as the Oracle called out two names rather than one. A Hakron warrior? She glanced at Aki as he kneeled down on her right and then at the unknown male who took up the station on her left. His mind flowed toward hers in a soothing stream and she took a quick glance at his face. Gods, he was beautiful and a perfect foil to the blondness of Aki.

"I..." Elli stuttered.

"You have something to say, Elli Slavin?" the Oracle asked.

Having been humiliated at one mating ceremony, Elli was determined not to be made a fool of again.

"With all due respect, Oracle, I was not expecting two mates."

The Hakron warrior's hopeful expression disappeared and beside her Aki stirred as if he was about to protest.

"You object to this pairing?"

"I—" Elli stared into the anguished grey eyes of the unknown male. "May I speak to him for a second?"

The Oracle's daughter spoke. "You doubt the Oracle's choice for you?"

Elli risked a glance upward at the Oracle as the crowds around them muttered and whispered. "I have been disappointed once before."

"That is true. You may speak to him," the Oracle decreed.

Aki touched her shoulder and murmured. "Elli, this is the Hakron warrior I told you about."

"The one you met on your journey to the Temple?"

"Aye." Aki looked rueful. "The one you told me not to mention so as to not complicate things."

"*Oh...*" Elli breathed. She turned to her other side and held out her hand to the quietly waiting Hakron warrior. "Do you think you are mated to Aki?"

"Aye, I do. The Oracle foretold the coming of the two warriors from another time to my brother and me on our eighteenth birthday. We have waited ten years for the prophecy to be fulfilled." He held her gaze. "But if you do not want to consider me, as a your Second, I will not contest your choice. I wish you and Aki to have every happiness in this world."

She pushed against his mental barriers and he let her in without protest. His mind blended seamlessly into hers offering her everything, hiding nothing. After a long moment she sighed. "Thank you."

"You are most welcome, Elli." His smile was as beautifully direct as his thoughts.

"Are we done now?" The Oracle cleared her throat. "Elli Slavin, I will ask you once again. Do you accept your mates, Aki and Morek?"

Elli took a long slow breath. If she wanted Aki--and Morek was certain his First Male had finally appeared--then she must be theirs. It made sense to her on a visceral level she had never believed in before. It was time to take a leap of faith and throw off her old fears. She nodded as both men took her hands in theirs.

"Yes. I accept them both."

The Oracle raised her hands. "With the power of the Gods within me, I bind you three to each other for all time. If this is not your wish, speak now or forever hold your peace."

"I object!"

A gasp ran around the room, and for a second, Elli thought she'd been pushed back into the past and that Carlin was speaking again. She risked a look down the stairs and blinked hard.

Carlin *was* standing there.

The Oracle's First Daughter clapped her hands. "This matter will be resolved in private. Everyone who is not involved may leave and continue to celebrate their own mating."

Elli winced as the crowd started to whisper and point at her. Why was this happening again? What the frak did Carlin *want*?

The Oracle beckoned for Carlin to approach the throne. "Why are you disrupting this most sacred of ceremonies?"

Carlin went down on one knee and kissed the Oracle's beringed finger. "I beg your forgiveness, Goddess, but I could not let this mating stand." He turned to Elli. "You were promised to *me*. I was named your First Male when you were eighteen."

Beside her Aki gave a low growl. "You lost her."

Carlin winced. "I was a fool. I allowed myself to believe the couple I met off-world were my true mates." He kept his gaze on Elli, his expression hopeful. "I don't want them anymore. I want *you*."

Elli shook her head, and Aki took her hand in a firmer grasp. "Elli is my female."

"And mine." The Hakron warrior took her other hand. She felt surrounded by their concern and love.

"We will not allow you to take her from us." There was a distinct threat in Aki's words.

The Oracle put a hand on his arm. "You will not fight within my sanctuary, Viking." She turned to Carlin. "You say this Triad of yours is irretrievably broken?"

"Yes, my lady."

"Where are the other two members?"

"They are currently in Pavlon City."

"Then we shall bring them here to find out their side of this story. Once I have spoken to them *I* will decide how to proceed."

Aki opened his mouth and then seemed to think better of arguing with a Goddess.

"We will reconvene this meeting as soon as they arrive

tomorrow." The Oracle studied them all. "I expect you all to behave yourselves in the meantime."

Everyone bowed as the Oracle left. As soon as she had gone, Aki took a menacing step toward Carlin and the Hakron male grabbed hold of him.

"Aki..."

Picking up her skirts, Elli ran down the steps and out of the sanctuary. Whispers and mutters followed her flight, and yet again she was an object of curiosity and pity. How dare Carlin turn up like some spoiled child expecting to get his own way again? It was so like him.

MOREK CLAMPED his hand down hard on Aki's shoulder. "Do not fight him. Promise me." He sent an urgent appeal to Einarr and Ungar who appeared in the doorway.

"Keep Aki safe. I will go and find Elli Slavin."

Einarr nodded and went to head his brother off while Morek went down the stairs, following Elli's scattered flight. Just that small glimpse of her thoughts and holding her hand had imprinted her indelibly in his mind. She was his mate. He no longer doubted that. Now all he had to do was find her and convince her that he and Aki would never give up their claim to her.

He traced her into one of the far-flung gardens where few visitors to the Temple ever ventured. Had she fled here the first time Carlin had humiliated her in public? She sat with her back against a stone wall, with her knees drawn up to her chin. A glint of tears remained in her eyes. Morek wanted to kill Carlin himself.

"Be my guest."

She looked up at him, and he dropped into a crouch beside her.

"He deserves killing," Morek remarked. "But I suspect Aki would be the first in line to accomplish that task. I left Einarr and Ungar holding him back."

She sighed. "I just want to run away right now."

"I can quite understand why." He took her hand and gently squeezed it. "By the way, my name is Morek. I am your Second Male."

She searched his face. "Why would you want to be that when all I do is create embarrassment for everyone?"

"Because you are my Female." He held her gaze and gently cupped her chin. "I can already feel you in my mind." He reached for her in his head. "Can you feel me?"

She swallowed hard. "I'm not sure if I want to make any more connections today. I can't bear the thought that I'll mess you up as well."

"I am more than willing to bear your pain, my lady. Aki and I have already agreed that whatever the Oracle says, we consider ourselves to be your males for as long as we all shall live."

"That's… very sweet of you."

"My thoughts are not entirely sweet," Morek confessed. "I cannot help but imagine what it will be like to share your bed."

Her pupils widened, and she licked her lips. "Don't say that."

"Why not?"

"Because now you've got me imagining things and thanks to stupid Carlin they might not happen."

Morek held her gaze. "They will happen, Elli. I promise you that. By tomorrow night if you so desire it you will be naked and in bed with Aki and me. I cannot wait."

He used his thumb to wipe away the salty tracks of her tears. "You will need to be strong today, my lady, and have faith that by tomorrow everything will be resolved to your satisfaction. The Oracle is wise. She will not fail us."

She took a deep breath and finally smiled at him. "I damn well hope so."

He took one of the perfumed white flowers out of his braided hair and placed it gently behind her ear. In her own way she was as much a warrior as he and Aki. "That's the spirit, my Female."

He rose to his feet and held out his hand. "May I escort you back to the Temple? The Oracle wishes you to stay with her handmaidens this evening."

"Thank you." She put her hand in his and faced him. "Thank you for everything."

"I did nothing but reassure you of that you already know in your heart. Aki and I are yours for all eternity."

She slowly went up on tiptoe to kiss his mouth.

Morek allowed the kiss to remain as platonic as she wished. He had no doubt that she would soon come willingly to him and Aki, and that the Oracle would make a decision that would destroy all Carlin's foolish dreams.

AFTER DEPOSITING Elli back with the Oracle's handmaidens, Morek made his way to the guest quarters where Aki was staying with his brother. When he arrived he wasn't surprised to find his First Male pacing the floor, his expression furious, his dagger in his hand.

"Did you find her?" Aki demanded.

"Aye, she is safely within the sanctuary now."

"Thank the Gods," Aki breathed. "Is she all right?"

Morek grimaced. "She is mortified and believes you and I would do well to stay away from her."

Aki stopped pacing. "You told her that wouldn't happen? That we were hers whatever the Oracle said?"

"I did. I believe she was beginning to accept that we meant it by the time I left her."

"If I could just stab that fool through the heart...."

"And be banished for desecrating a holy shrine to our Goddess?" Morek shook his head. "That would hardly help our cause."

"Then what do you suggest?"

Morek spread his hands wide. "That we rely on the Oracle to make the correct decision tomorrow. I have faith that she will."

Aki collapsed into a chair and put his head in his hands. "By all that is holy, I hope you are right."

Morek moved over to touch his bowed head. "By all that is holy, so do I."

7

____

AKI ALLOWED MOREK TO HELP HIM DRESS AND THEN FOLLOWED his mate down to the inner sanctum of the Temple. There weren't many people about on the terraces. It was late afternoon, and the temperature was high and the shadows long. His thoughts were fixed on Elli, who seemed to be hiding behind her superior shields. But even she couldn't hide completely from him anymore. Morek had explained that mated couples shared more deeply than was common, and Aki now knew that was true.

At the door to the Oracle's private apartments, the two men stopped and Morek wrapped his arm around Aki's shoulders.

"We must believe that the Oracle will make the correct decision."

"But what if she doesn't?" Aki argued. "What will we do then?"

Morek's eyes were troubled. "I cannot imagine disobeying the Oracle, but in this instance when I am certain in my soul that Elli is our mate, I admit I am conflicted." He nodded decisively. "I will do whatever you wish, First Male, but I will not let you kill this Carlin."

"Agreed," Aki said. He brushed a kiss on Morek's forehead. "Let's pray it doesn't come to that."

The Oracle was seated at an oval table and beckoned to the men to join her. She wore her usual white robe and her long auburn hair was held back from her face with a crown of flowers.

"Aki and Morek sit on my right. Carlin and his Triad members on my left, please, and Elli take the place opposite me."

Everyone sat down, and Aki took a covert glance at the couple sitting opposite him. They looked upset and were holding hands, their bodies turned toward each other and away from Carlin who sat stiffly beside them.

The Oracle inclined her head and began speaking. "Ilic and Tria, thank you for coming to my Temple at Quoxor. I am hoping that you can clarify the situation between you and Carlin."

The male bowed. "Thank you, Goddess. Carlin believes he made a mistake in choosing to mate with us. We do not agree with his decision, but he refuses to honor his commitment to us."

Aki snorted and muttered under his breath to Morek. "See? He is a man who has no morals and lacks loyalty."

Morek elbowed him to be quiet.

"Carlin? What do you have to say about this?" the Oracle asked.

Carlin shifted uncomfortably in his seat. "They want to have children. I don't." She continued to look at him expectantly, and he frowned. "What else do you want me to say, my lady?"

"Surely such matters can be talked out with the aid of a counselor?"

"Carlin refused to seek help. He said that his decision was irreversible," the female Tria spoke up. "We tried *everything...*"

"Then you should have presented yourself as a Triad at the Temple here and asked for my counsel."

Tria nodded. "That's what we thought Carlin was here for. We didn't know he was planning to disrupt another mating."

"Ah." The Oracle's gaze swept over Elli. "Then Carlin's presence here at this moment was an unhappy coincidence."

She went silent, and Aki held her breath as she considered.

"Carlin, I intend to dissolve your Triad. Not for your benefit, but for your two mates who have been treated very badly." She glanced over at her daughter Neeve, who was listening intently. "Draw up the proclamation, First Daughter, and make sure it is announced to the Temple guests this very evening."

She bowed to Ilic and Tria. "I wish you both well in your lives and can assure you that your union will be long, prosperous *and* fruitful." Her smile was beautiful. "If you linger in the lower Temple and ask one of my handmaidens to introduce you to a man named Wren, I believe you will all be very happy together."

The couple rose from their chairs and came to kneel at the Oracle's feet. Tria was crying openly now. "Thank you, Goddess. Thank you so much."

Neeve escorted them out of the room, and the door was shut behind them. Aki tried to relax, but he had a sense that things weren't resolved yet.

"So you are setting me free so that I can reclaim my place as Elli's First Male?" Carlin asked.

Aki growled low in his throat and cracked his knuckles, wishing he'd been allowed to bring his dagger into the room. Morek patted his arm soothingly.

"No, Carlin. I am setting your Triad partners free of you." The Oracle paused. "The only person who has to make a decision at this point is Elli Slavin."

All eyes turned to Elli who sat frozen at the foot of the table.

"It is only fitting that *Elli* gets to make her own decision is it not?" the Oracle asked. "She is the one who has been publicly embarrassed *twice* by the behavior of her males."

Aki slowly stood up, his heart hammering like Thor in his chest.

"Yes, Viking?"

"I agree with your decision, Goddess." He looked down the table at Elli. "I think Elli has a right to choose to become part of a Triad—or not."

Morek nodded and rose to stand shoulder to shoulder with Aki. "And I agree with Aki."

"You would both give her up if she preferred to be free?"

"Aye," Morek said.

Aki grimaced. "I would never stop loving her, but having been trapped myself for four thousand years, I wish her to be free."

Carlin shot to his feet. "I don't agree. Elli needs to abide by her original promise to *me*."

The Oracle smiled at Elli. "The choice is yours, my dear. If you don't wish to mate with any of them, just say the word and I will make it so."

As Elli stood up, Aki held his breath.

She inclined her head respectfully to the Oracle. "I would like to be mated to Aki and Morek."

"Then that's what shall happen." The Oracle raised her voice and held out her hands. "With the power of the Gods within me, I bind you three to each other for all time."

Aki felt the force of her power sear through him and the sense of bonding with his two mates as though their very thoughts were welded into one complex strand. Morek grabbed his hand, only emphasizing the connection and they both rocked on their feet.

When he opened his eyes, Aki felt the Oracle's mind brush against his.

"I give you permission to dispose of the unwanted one, Viking."

With a savage smile, Aki pushed back his chair and advanced upon Carlin who was still whining about how unfair everything was. When he saw Aki coming, he tried to run but he was no match for an enraged Viking. Scooping him up by the throat, Aki picked him up and strode out of the room and down the stairs into the most public of the Temple chambers.

Holding Carlin over his head he dropped him into the depths of one of the ornamental ponds surrounding the series of fountains. The onlookers clapped and laughed as if Aki was part of a traveling show.

When Carlin resurfaced and sat on his arse coughing up water, Aki leaned close.

"Do not trouble my Female again *Kukalabbi!*"

He dusted off his hands and walked away.

SEVERAL HOURS LATER, Elli was sitting in her bedroom nervously brushing her hair. She and Aki and Morek had eaten a leisurely meal together and then sat and talked on the verandah until they'd joined Einarr and his mates for a double celebration. Now the two groups had separated again, and Aki and Morek were waiting patiently outside to see whether she had the nerve to admit them into her bed.

They probably weren't aware just how nervous she was. Having only spent one night with Aki, her skill set wasn't advanced. The thought of having *two* virile warriors in her bed at once was remarkably daunting.

But she'd accepted them as her mates. She *wanted* them, so why was she so worried? All she had to do was be honest. They would understand. Taking a deep breath, she opened the door and went into the small chamber between her and Aki's rooms.

It was empty.

So much for them waiting eagerly for her summons. Elli wanted to smile.

She heard a murmur of voices, and gathering her courage,

went through Aki's door and stopped short. Morek sat on the bed clad in nothing but his long dark hair, and Aki was in the middle of shedding his clothes.

"Oh!" Elli blurted out. "I didn't mean to intrude." Perhaps they'd decided not to wait for her at all and were making their own fun.

"Intrude on what?" Aki's head emerged from his shirt leaving him just in unlaced black pants. Elli checked to see that her tongue was safely inside her mouth and she wasn't drooling. "We were just debating how many clothes we should wear when we came to your bedchamber."

Morek slipped off the bed. "We were not intending on starting without you, Elli. Please do not think that."

She held up her hands. Morek was far too astute to miss anything. "That's okay, actually, that's kind of what I came in here to say and—"

Aki's smile disappeared. "What's wrong?"

She stared at them helplessly, her tongue tied in knots.

"*Elli?*"

Morek took one hand and Aki took the other, and she just let the jumble of her thoughts fall into their minds. Sometimes being a telepath was incredibly useful.

"Ah." Morek nodded. "There is no rush, my Female. We have the whole of our lives to make love together."

"He's right," Aki said. "Mayhap tonight we should just try sleeping in the same bed?"

"Won't you be disappointed?" Elli asked. "And I don't mind if you and Morek want to… you know, in fact I'd quite like to see how that works."

Gods she was babbling again. It seemed that she'd shed her calm and cool persona right along with her past.

"You would?" Aki asked.

Morek chuckled. "Aki has four thousand years of fucking to make up for. He is a little more impatient than I am." He kissed

Elli's hand. "But if you wish to see us, I would be delighted to show you."

Aki put his arm around her. "How about we just go to bed first and see how we feel?"

Morek was already naked and Elli couldn't help notice that he was fully aroused. His cock wasn't quite as large as Aki's, but it was still substantial. Aki took off his pants, and then they both looked expectantly at Elli, who clutched the lapels of her robe even harder to her chest.

"Come." Aki climbed up into the large bed and patted the sheet beside him. Elli went after him, shedding her robe to reveal the large T-shirt underneath. Morek got in after her and for a while they sorted out whose arm went where until Elli found herself practically lying across the two men.

It felt wonderful.

Her eyes started to close as Aki stroked her hair back from her face, and Morek wrapped an arm around her hips, turning her slightly on her side. His thick cock rubbed against her lower back, and Aki's was within reach of her bent right knee. Both of them were aroused but neither of them made any attempt to push inside her.

They understood. Why had she even doubted them?

When she woke up later, the moon was bright, her T-shirt had gone and she was rubbing herself against Aki's broad thigh while he stroked her ass with his fingers in long lazy circles. She wasn't even sure if he was awake, but she didn't want him to stop.

Morek's fingers slid down from her waist and he cupped her sex.

"So beautiful, so wet."

She arched against him, and he began to play with her clit and circle around her swollen folds until she was pushing down on him with every stroke.

"Elli."

That was Aki in her mind, his lips moving over her throat and then down to capture her taut nipple in his mouth, which only doubled her excitement. Morek added more fingers as he rocked against her, the wet path of his cock branding her lower back with every thrust.

"More?" Aki murmured as he licked his way down over her stomach and then, Gods, his tongue was tangling with Morek's fingers and she was coming in great shuddering gasps. She clutched Aki's hair and heard Morek's low laugh behind her as she silently begged for more.

Aki's tongue licked her clit once more. *"Will you take Morek inside you?"*

"Yes."

"Let me hold you. I want to see you both," Aki commanded as he rolled onto his back and sat up, drawing Elli between his legs, his cock pressed against her spine. Morek shoved the bedclothes out of the way and crouched between her spread thighs, his hair hanging over one shoulder, and his focus entirely on her.

He smoothed a hand over his cock and then rubbed the crown very gently against Elli's already sensitized clit.

"I have never made love to a Female before. I am afraid I will disappoint you."

Elli fought a smile. "I've only made love with Aki for one night. I would say that our inexperience is similar."

Aki's low chuckle made them both glance at him. "Then perhaps you should both learn from me?" He nodded at Morek. "Just take your time and let her mind guide you into what pleases her."

Morek nodded and swallowed hard. "Watch me, Elli. Watch me become yours."

Aki's fingers came down to rest over her stomach, the longest just touching the top of her clit. When Morek started to ease in, Aki played with her, distracting her from the thrust of

Morek's solid column of flesh, setting off nerve endings that made her crave the penetration so desperately that she was soon whimpering with need.

"Aye, that's my Female. Take all of him," Aki breathed.

Morek groaned and reached a hand out to brace himself on Aki's shoulder. "That is…" His words ended and his mind took over showing Elli and Aki his feelings from their source. His wonder in their acceptance made Elli want to wrap her arms and legs around him and never let him go.

"One day," Aki whispered. "When you are used to both of us, you'll take both of us, aye? Mouth or arse or…"

Elli shivered through a climax.

"You like that idea, don't you?" Aki kissed her throat. "Not half as much as I do. I can't wait to have Morek while he has you."

"Or vice versa," Morek groaned. "Gods, if you keep talking Aki Bloodaxe I'm going to come."

"Don't let me stop you, Second Male. Elli does need her sleep you know."

Morek exhaled and shoved forward one last time, his hot come jetting deep within Elli. "Thank you my Female. Thank you."

His climax set Elli off again and she held him tightly until he finally stopped moving over her. He felt different from Aki both physically and telepathically, but still recognizably hers. She breathed the mingled scent of their lovemaking and thought there wasn't a better scent in the whole universe. She suspected she'd never get tired of it. This was what it meant to be so integrated with her mated pair that every single thing about them became precious and special and irreplaceable.

Morek pulled out of her and rolled onto his side and closed his eyes. "I think I am close to paradise."

Aki slid his fingers into Morek's long hair and pulled gently.

"Not until you've finished your obligations to your new mates. My cock needs some attention."

Elli licked her lips. "I could help him out with that."

Behind her Aki went still.

"Are you sure, my heart? Morek and I don't want to tire you out."

"But I want to."

Before she even finished speaking, she was lifted off Aki's lap, turned around and placed on her knees facing him. Morek joined her and they both studied Aki's huge cock.

"He needs a lot of attention," Morek finally said. "We can take it in turns, aye? So that neither of us get tired."

"Agreed." Elli leaned in and licked a drip of pre-cum off Aki's crown. "After you."

She suddenly wasn't sleepy anymore. She watched the way Morek used his mouth to torment Aki into muttering unintelligible Norse curses that even her translator couldn't decipher. If she was lucky, and not too sore, she might persuade Aki to make love to her later. She wanted him very much.

Morek turned to smile at her, and she kissed his smooth green cheek. She was where she wanted to be. She had *chosen* to be there and for the first time since Carlin's desertion, she could finally be herself.

And that, in her mind, was the greatest prize of all.

The End

A NOTE TO READERS

Dear Readers,

We met one four thousand year old Viking in *Viking Unbound*, so it's only fair that his twin brother gets his own book. *Viking Claimed* deals with Aki, Einarr's twin brother. You also got to meet other familiar characters from the *Triad* series as our two fearless Vikings find their happy ever after's.

If you enjoyed this book, please consider leaving a review at your favorite retailer.

If you want to read more of my books, please check out my website and consider joining my newsletter for the fastest updates and early contests to win new books.

katepearce.com/newsletter

Thank you for reading!
Kate Pearce

Continue the series with *The Power of Fate*...

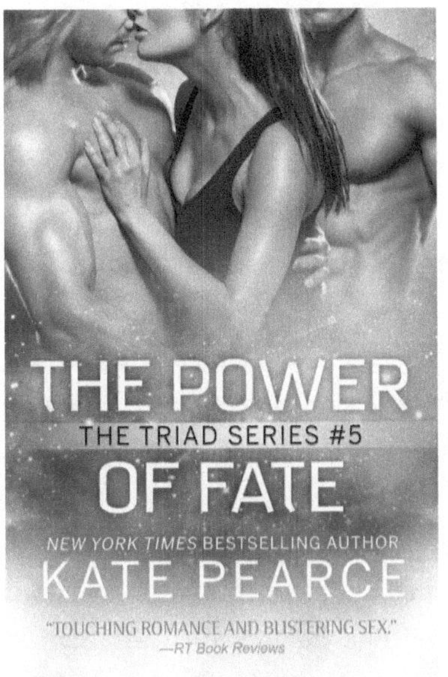

Chapter One

"Mya, pay attention!"

"I *am*..." Her breath hissed out as Orin expertly kicked with his bare foot, caught her shoulder, and sent her flying backward onto the black exercise mat.

He came down over her, the side of his hand slicing across her throat. "You'd be dead now if this were real."

She grinned up at him. "But it isn't, and you wouldn't kill me."

His expression remained serious. "This isn't funny. I'm trying to make sure you are one hundred percent ready to go on this mission."

"This was supposed to be fun." She shoved at his chest, but he didn't budge a centimeter. "Orin..."

After a second he rolled off her and stalked over to the side of the mat. "I picked up another shift tonight. I need to go shower."

For a long, stunned moment, Mya remained on her back staring up at the ceiling before following Orin up the stairs to the bathroom in their apartment. Clouds of steam issued out of the shower.

"Hey."

He was naked and just about to step into the shower.

"You're going out on my last night home?" She tried to keep her tone light, but she had an absurd desire to cry. He stepped under the water, and she focused on his assured movements as he lathered himself with soap and washed his short black hair.

"Orin..."

She sank down onto the side of the bath as he ignored her. Tentatively, she probed his mind, but his shields were up. It was like scraping her fingernails against a metal door. They'd been mated for ten years. What the frak was happening?

"Please talk to me, Orin."

He kept his back to her and his mind closed. Wearily, she got up and went to the spare bedroom and showered there. She was quick because she was not going to allow him to leave without talking to her properly. Wrapping the towel around herself, she went back into their bedroom where he was dressing in his city police uniform. She took a deep breath.

"Is there someone else?"

He stopped moving but kept his back to her. "Mya, that's stupid. We're mated. I don't do casual sex."

"So you're just tired of me?"

He slowly turned. "I'm tired of this distance between us."

"You're the one who put it there, Orin."

He pulled a thin protective vest over his black T-shirt, his movements jerky and impatient. "Do you really want to do this just before you leave on a mission?"

"Why not?" She raised her chin. "Better than leaving things to fester. Maybe being away will give me a chance to think about what's wrong and work out how *I* feel. I don't *want* to fight with you."

"You don't want to fight about anything. You're Hakron. You think everything can be sorted out with prayer and goodwill."

"Even though I chose to join the military, there's nothing wrong with promoting peace. It has prevented bloodshed in my tribe for hundreds of years."

He sank down on the side of the bed and stared at his booted feet. "We've been mated for a decade."

She nodded even though he wasn't looking at her. "And?"

"You won't talk about changing that. I want to take you to the Temple at Quoxor and find out who our Third is." He looked up, his blue gaze utterly serious. "I want a child."

Only mated Triads could conceive children on their planet. And only the Oracle could sanction a bonded Triad—not that Mya was sure that she'd ever be ready for a child.

"But we agreed that we'd wait until both our careers were stable, and this mission is crucial to me proving I'm the obvious choice to take over for Major Esca." She was almost stuttering in her haste to remind him. "We discussed this. I thought you *agreed* with me."

"That was before all this shit went down at work." His throat worked. "Before Kran died."

Mya sank down to her knees in front of him. "Losing your partner like that was horrible, Orin."

"It made me think. What if I go next? I'd be leaving you alone and without even a child to remember me by." He held up his hand. "And don't tell me you'd manage—that you'd be fine without me. I know that. You're a strong woman."

"You make it sound as if I wouldn't miss you at all." Mia's words stuck in her throat. "I'm your mate. I'd be *devastated*. You make it sound like I don't care."

"I don't mean that." He shoved a hand through his now spiky hair. "This is about *me*, not you. *I've* changed. I *know* what we said—what we agreed. And I know you're frightened. All I'm asking you to do is think about it, okay? If you don't want a child—maybe, just maybe, our Third might?"

She remained kneeling, staring at nothing as her carefully constructed world collapsed around her. If she wouldn't give him a child he'd get one another way.

Without her.

With a Third.

Yeah, and that always worked out *so* well…

"I do love you, Mya. In a perfect world, all I'd want is a child with you. You are my heart." Orin spoke so quietly she almost couldn't hear him.

She closed her eyes and took a deep breath. She would not fight with him. She would *not*. "I love you, too. Keep safe tonight. When I get back, I promise we can talk about this some more."

"That's—" He paused as relief flooded his even features. "*Thank you.* Thank you so much. If we did have a child, I'd stay home with it and our Third, I wouldn't expect you to be at home if you wanted to stay in the military."

Pushing her out, making her obsolete to his happiness… "You've obviously thought about this quite a bit."

He shrugged. "I had a lot of time when I was stuck in that hospital bed recovering."

She managed a nod. It was pretty much all she could dredge up at this moment. His wrist com beeped and he cursed.

"Gotta go."

"Okay," Mya whispered. "Take care of yourself and come back safely to me."

"I'll do my best." His com beeped again. Ignoring it, he put his hands on her shoulders. "I love you, Mya. Please don't forget that. I want what's best for both of us, not just me, I swear it."

She nodded again as his mind reached for hers, and for a long moment, their thoughts tangled and blended until he eased back.

"Maybe I should call in sick," he murmured as he cupped her cheek. "I don't want to leave you. I'm a frakking idiot to have started this right now."

"I'm good." She summoned another smile. "Really. I have to leave in less than two hours, so you might as well go and earn that overtime."

"Are you sure?"

Leaning in, she kissed his firm mouth. "Yes. Go. Be well."

He reluctantly let her go, his worried blue gaze fixed on hers as he picked up his heavy jacket and backed toward the door. "I love you. Stay safe, you hear?"

"Shouldn't be a problem. This is just an escort mission."

"To an Etruscan moon. So be careful."

"I always am."

"Which is why you'll get that promotion." He blew her a kiss. "Let me know how things are going when you can."

"Will do."

She stayed where she was until the door of their apartment slammed behind him. There was no point hanging around feeling sorry for herself. She might as well get to the base and prepare for the mission ahead. Most of her gear was already packed. She just needed to put on her uniform.

She went to get up and couldn't; her arms wrapped around her waist as tears fell in an endless stream. Gods it *hurt*. She used her towel to mop up the storm of weeping and tried to talk herself into a better frame of mind. Orin wanted to find their Third and have a child, which was totally natural and understandable.

Both of those things *terrified* her.

He *knew* that. At least some of it.

It was her fault for starting the whole damn conversation.

She'd practically begged him to tell her what was wrong. Just because she didn't like his answer didn't make Orin's feelings any less valid or important. At least he'd tried to be honest with her.

He did love her. She knew that in her soul.

Usually, getting dressed in her uniform helped her collect her thoughts, but tonight it proved impossible. How could she have misinterpreted Orin's increasing withdrawal from her so badly? She was his mate, and yet he'd managed to hide the extent of his feelings for months because she was so busy chasing that promotion.

But he knew how important it was to her, which was probably why he'd hidden his issues so well. If she gained the rank of major she'd be the first Hakron female to ever reach that grade in the Pavlovan Special Forces. She studied her pale green reflection in the mirror. But was her ambition worth losing her best friend and lover over?

If she deliberately stepped back and didn't seek the promotion, would she end up resenting Orin? Could she even *carry* a baby without losing her mind during the pregnancy? She didn't know. And the thought of a Third… Shouldering her pack, she headed for the door. All she could do was honor her promise to Orin, think things through while she was away, and come back ready to have another honest discussion. She hadn't told him how bad things really were in her family because it was still too painful to talk about. Perhaps it was time to trust him with all of it.

She loved him. She'd promised him she'd try.

There was nothing more important than that.

An hour later, she was at the military base checking in with her team when her superior officer stepped out of his office and called her name.

"Captain Jong?"

Mya saluted. "Yes, sir?"

"Do you have a moment?"

She followed Major Esca into his office and shut the door. He took his seat behind the desk and folded his hands in front of him. Her superior officer was paler than usual, the bags under his eyes more pronounced. Even his black hair had dulled. Worn to the bone—exactly as could be expected from a man whose mate had been injured. Mya was sure she'd looked the same for the weeks Orin was in the hospital. They all knew that Major Esca's First Male, Ash, who basically ran the Pavlovan Senate, had been injured in an Etruscan attack that had also affected several Hakron villagers. Senator Ash was still recuperating at home, and the Major had been running himself ragged trying to do his job and take care of his mate.

"Jong, I wanted you to be the first to know that I'm leaving this position." A shot of pure adrenaline shook through her as he looked up at her. "I am recommending you for promotion. I can't think of anyone who could fill my shoes as well as you could."

"Thank you, sir." Mya swallowed hard and saluted. This was what she'd been working so hard to achieve, and his words gave her immense satisfaction. But the thought that she was achieving her goal because her superior officer's mate was suffering didn't sit well with her. "That is very good of you."

"I can't guarantee you'll get the job, but with my connections, it's pretty damn likely."

Mya tried to smile. "May I ask what you intend to do next, sir?"

Major Esca sat back and stretched out his legs. "When Senator Ash is recovered, I'm going to be spearheading the development of a new security team to protect the leaders of our Senate. We've had too many close calls recently—what with the attack on the Temple at Quoxor, the attempted abduction of the Oracle, *and* the bringing down of Senator Ash's plane."

"The Etruscans are definitely getting bolder."

"And we're going to have to consider what to do about that on a larger scale soon. No one wants an outright war, but these acts of aggression are getting out of hand."

"Agreed, sir."

"The mission we are about to undertake is twofold. There is a diplomatic side where our ambassador is going to lay it on the line to the Etruscans, and there is a 'fact gathering' element. While I'm facing off with the Etruscans and trying to keep my temper, you and your team will be assessing the Etruscan moon. We've never been close enough to get a good sense of it before, let alone been allowed on the surface, and it could be strategically important if we do end up at war."

"Understood."

"You will be discreet and invisible."

"Aren't I always, sir?"

His smile was more like his old self. "I'm relying on that. Be careful, Jong."

End of Sample
To continue reading, be sure to pick up The Power of Fate at your favorite retailer.

ALSO BY KATE PEARCE

The Diable Delamere Series

Historical Romance

Regency dukes, disinherited aristocrats and a plot to assassinate the Prince Regent create plenty of problems for all the heroes and heroines as they struggle to trust each other in an ever-changing game of love, deceit and treachery.

The Millcastle Series

Historical Romance

On the cusp of the industrial revolution in the northern town of Millcastle the old and the new clash both in matters of business and of the heart. Can love flourish among the rush to make a profit?

House of Pleasure / Simply Series

Historical Erotic Romance

Enter a Regency house of pleasure where nothing is forbidden and every sexual desire you have ever imagined can come true...

The Sinners Club

Historical Erotic Romance

When intrigue collides with heated passion behind the closed doors of the Sinners Club there is nowhere left to hide.

.

The Morgan Ranch Series

Contemporary Western Romance

A Northern Californian ranching family torn apart by tragedy reluctantly return home to discover not everything was as they thought it was, and that love, and forgiveness can sometimes go hand in hand.

.

The Millers of Morgan Valley Series

Contemporary Western Romance

When the mother you haven't seen for twenty years asks to visit your family ranch and set the record straight, how will her ex and six adult children react? The loves and sometimes messy lives of a ranching family.

.

The Turner Brothers

Contemporary Erotic Western Romance

Three half-brothers find their own uniquely passionate ways to find the loves of their lives and accept exactly who they are—no holds barred.

.

The Obsidian Series

Sci-Fi Romance

Join a renegade band of telepaths roaming the galaxy to protect and rescue their race from the evil empire intent on destroying them.

.

Planet Valhalla Series

Sci-Fi/Futuristic Erotic Romance

One human female crash lands on a planet full of men descended from the Vikings, one of whom is the King who claims her as his mate—what could possibly go wrong? A sexy romp through the stars with excessive sex, a touch of humor and some very satisfied women…

.

The Triad Series

Sci-Fi/Futuristic Erotic Romance

Welcome to an imaginary world where civilizations, clash against the new and unknown, where telepaths are revered and reviled, and where your destiny can be preordained by a living oracle. Add in a group of super-soldier telepaths rescued from Earth and forming sexual triads for life becomes even more complex and life changing.

.

The Tribute Series

Sci-Fi/Futuristic *Dark* Erotic Romance

To save their planet from extinction the government will demand everything from the condemned few—willingly or not.

"Fans of no-holds-barred erotic portrayals of non- and quasi-consensual encounters will devour this steamy triptych."

– Publishers Weekly

Soul Justice Series

Paranormal Romance

Come and join a San Francisco based secret government department who investigate the monsters under the bed while risking their psychic abilities and even their own lives.

The Tudor Vampire Chronicles

Paranormal Historical Romance

Druids, Vampires and the court of King Henry VIII and his many wives form the backbone of this intriguing series as good fights evil through the first ever female Vampire slayer of her line, Rosalind Llewellyn.

Kurland St. Mary Mysteries

Historical Mystery

Writing as Catherine Lloyd

Join wounded cavalry hero Major Sir Robert Kurland and Lucy Harrington the rector's eldest daughter as they solve crimes in their quiet little village and gradually learn to appreciate each other.

ABOUT KATE PEARCE

New York Times and *USA Today* bestselling author Kate Pearce was born in England in the middle of a large family of girls and quickly found that her imagination was far more interesting than real life. After acquiring a degree in history and barely escaping from the British Civil Service alive, she moved to California and then to Hawaii with her kids and her husband and set about reinventing herself as a romance writer.

She is known for both her unconventional heroes and her joy at subverting romance clichés. In her spare time she self publishes science fiction erotic romance, historical romance, and whatever else she can imagine. You can find Kate at katepearce.com.

amazon.com/author/katepearce
goodreads.com/katepearce
bookbub.com/authors/kate-pearce
facebook.com/KatePearceAuthor
twitter.com/kate4queen